Falling Slowly

Lila Bruce

Falling Slowly

Falling Slowly

ISBN 13: 978-1503223202

ISBN 10: 1503223205

Original Publication Date: November 2014

With appreciation to Shelby, for helping me to get off the ground

and

To Mimi and Connie-Susan...You both have another thing coming

Chapter One

There was a cat on her pillow.

Quinn didn't have anything against cats, really, but had always considered herself to be more of a dog person. Not that she had ever owned a dog, but, if asked, she would say that she preferred dogs over cats. There was just something about a cat that was unsettling. The way they looked at a person with their almond-shaped eyes.

The way the calico cat was looking at her now.

"If you think I'm giving you this pillow, then you better think again," Quinn said to the cat. The cat looked at Quinn as if she understood the words fully, narrowing her eyes and giving a soft—and slightly threatening—meow. Quinn stared back, ready to stand her ground, or lie on it—whatever.

Beep-Beep-Beep-Beep.

The shrill sound of the alarm clock suddenly pierced the stillness of the room, interrupting the showdown over ownership of the pillow.

Quinn frowned and raised her head, glancing over at the alarm clock.

6:01 a.m. *Damn it.*

With a sigh Quinn reached across to the small black lacquer table that sat beside her bed and silenced the alarm. She tossed back a dark blue quilt and sat up. As she did, the calico cat moved forward, taking full possession of the pillow.

"Don't get too comfortable," she said to the cat. "This isn't over yet." In response, the cat yawned and curled up in the warm spot vacated by Quinn's head.

Quinn twisted her lips at the cat as she swung her legs around and sat up on the side of the bed. As much as she would have liked to stay in bed for at least a few more hours, there was a lot to do and she was already behind. She stood, placing the bulk of her weight on her right foot, and stretched her body, groaning softly as she worked out the kinks in the stiff muscles of her back and arms. She padded out of the bedroom and headed toward the kitchen, the hardwood floor cold against her bare feet.

Sunlight was beginning to peek through the small window above the sink. Quinn looked out into the quickly receding darkness as she filled a glass carafe with water. She grimaced as she felt a familiar warmth begin to circulate in her left ankle.

It's going to be a long day.

She switched off the water and strode across the kitchen to start the coffee, ignoring the sharp sting of pain that radiated up her leg and down into her left foot with every step. She filled the reservoir and switched on the machine, then turned and headed back to the bedroom. After a quick shower and pulling on a pair of jeans and t-shirt, she made a failed attempt to straighten that one stubborn auburn curl that always refused to go down without a fight, and made her way back into the kitchen to pour the now percolated coffee into her favorite mug. Quinn sat at the table and began to flip through a magazine as she sipped her coffee.

The silence was broken as the android phone lying on the table began to light up and sing to her about a lost shaker of salt.

"Good morning, Rebekah," Quinn said into the phone, still sipping coffee.

"Are you up yet?" came the shrill reply.

"Nope, I'm still in bed sound asleep." Quinn loved her younger sister, but it was way too early in the morning to get caught up in whatever drama Rebekah had planned for the day. Four years younger than Quinn, Rebekah was also the exact opposite. While Quinn liked to think of herself as a calm, easy-going, and generally well put together person, her sister was…well…not so much.

"You don't have to be that way Quinn. And don't tell me to call back after you've had your coffee. You know how important this is to me today. I cannot be late," Rebekah said frantically. Quinn couldn't help but smile as she took the last swig of coffee and stood up from the table. She cocked the phone between her head and shoulder as she limped to the sink and rinsed out the mug before placing it upside down on a small wooden rack sitting on the countertop.

"I'm up, had my coffee, about to go find my shoes and keys and then I'll be over to pick you up. Don't worry, you're not going to be late," she said, walking into the living room. "Seriously, isn't it about time you got that car fixed, or maybe start looking for a new one?"

"Oh my gosh, can we not have this discussion right now? I am less than two hours away from the biggest meeting of my professional life. I don't need any extra stress, Quinn!"

"If I continue to stand here and talk to you rather than get ready, then you most definitely will be late. Ten minutes. I need ten minutes to finish putting myself together and then I'm out the door and headed that way." With that, she slipped the phone from her shoulder, hit the END button, and tossed it into the purse hanging off the end of the couch.

“Shoes, shoes, shoes,” she muttered as she glanced around the living room, finally locating the ankle length boots sitting neatly in a corner.

Quinn slipped the boots on, grabbed her purse, and headed out the door. The sun was peeking out and rising, the sky a dark pinkish orange. The chilly mid-March morning caused Quinn to shiver slightly as she slid into the late model sedan.

Definitely should have picked up a jacket. Had Rebekah not rushed her, she thought, she would have checked the weather before running outside. Quinn sighed and backed out of her driveway, flipping the heat on and the radio up. The husky vocals of Joss Stone filled the car as she turned onto the main road. It was still early, so there was little to no traffic as she made her way to her sister’s townhome on the other side of the county.

Way too early to be up on a Saturday morning.

She couldn’t help but keep the thought rolling through her head as she slowed for a red light. But, here she was, up and out at six-thirty in the morning to ferry her younger sister off to her latest endeavor. Of course, she was proud of Rebekah. No matter how many times she failed at something – and that was a lot – she always got back up and started again. Her latest venture was actually off to a promising start, with Rebekah landing a chance to display her handmade purses and jewelry in a chain of designer boutiques in the Atlanta area.

The light changed and she was on her way again. As if on cue, the phone in Quinn's purse began to light up and sing.

"Really Rebekah?" she said aloud, recognizing her sister's ringtone. "*So* not going to answer you."

Quinn continued to drive, ignoring the phone. After a moment, the ringing stopped.

She slowed the car as she neared Rebekah's townhome. Pulling into the driveway, she could see her sister looking out the front window. Quinn stopped the car as the lights in the townhome went off and the younger woman came bouncing out the front door juggling bags and boxes in her arms. Quinn stepped out of the car, frowning slightly at the spike of pain that came with putting pressure on her left ankle. She walked to the back and opened the trunk.

"Do you need some help?"

"Nope. I've got it."

Surely I did not hear a tone, Quinn thought.

"You've got it?"

"Yep, I've got it." With that Rebekah deposited the bags and boxes inside the trunk and then closed the lid. Loudly.

Quinn glanced at her sister sideways. The younger Briscoe sister stepped quickly to the front of the vehicle, opened the door, and threw herself into the front seat. She then closed the door. Loudly.

Really?

Quinn marched to the front of the car and repeated her sister's actions. She put the car in reverse and began to back out of the driveway. After a second of motion, she slammed on the brakes and put the vehicle back into park. She faced her sister.

"Is there something you want to say?"

"Is there something *you* want to say?"

"As a matter of fact, there is." Quinn could feel her blood pressure rising with each word. "I get that you're anxious about this meeting today, but do *not* take it out on me. I am up and out here at oh-dark-thirty on a Saturday morning to pick your ass up and haul it down to Atlanta when I could be still happily asleep in my nice warm bed, so do *not* give me attitude."

Rebekah opened her mouth in protest and then closed it.

"I'm sorry Quinn," she said. "I didn't mean to come off as ungrateful. I'm just really nervous about today. This opportunity is huge for me. If I can get picked up by this store, then that's just the beginning. Everything I have worked for and dreamed of for so long could finally be happening. I know how much I owe to you for supporting me."

Way to make me feel like a heel.

"I know you're grateful. Look, I know it's early and this is a huge day for you. Let's just both take a deep breath and get this road trip started."

"That's why you're so great Quinn."

"I know," Quinn said with a little laugh. She slid the sedan into reverse and backed out of the driveway and onto the road. The sun was fully up now and shining, causing Quinn to squint and pull down the sun visor.

"Look, we have plenty of time to get there," Quinn said. "What do you say we stop somewhere and get a bite to eat before your meeting? It'll help settle the butterflies in your stomach."

"That sounds great," Rebekah answered. "But let's wait 'til we get to Marietta just in case we run into traffic or something. I really don't want to be late."

"That's fine. I've had my coffee already this morning. To tell you the truth I've not been much a breakfast person here lately."

Out of the corner of her eye Quinn could see her sister cast a glance in her direction. She chose to ignore it as she turned onto the highway, heading south. Traffic was still light. But for the occasional passing eighteen-wheeler, theirs was the only car on the road.

"You know, I wasn't going to say anything, but I did notice that you look like you've lost some weight," Rebekah said.

Quinn held her gaze on the highway as she answered. "You say that like it's a bad thing."

"I'm not saying it's a bad thing."

"Then what are you saying?"

Rebekah shifted in her seat before she answered. "It's just...look, I know that things have been rough for you lately."

Quinn tightened her grip on the steering wheel. "Really? You know?" she said sarcastically.

"Okay, maybe I don't *know*, but you understand what I mean."

Quinn remained silent, continuing to focus on the highway.

After a long silence, Rebekah sighed and said, "Look, I'm really appreciative of your driving me down to meet with the boutique this morning. It may not be my place to say this, but we've been talking…"

"Who the fuck is we?" Quinn interrupted sharply.

“Me and Erin.”

Quinn scowled at the mention of their older sister.

“We really do care, Quinn. I’m not going to pretend to understand everything you’ve been through over the past couple of years, but I’m still your sister. You can try to shut me out all you want to, but I’m not going away.”

“I should be so lucky,” Quinn muttered under her breath.

“Whatever,” Rebekah said. “I know how hard you’ve worked to get things back to normal after your accident…”

“Accident?” Quinn snapped, raising one eyebrow and shaking her head. “Is that what we’re calling it these days?”

“Okay, then. I know how hard you’ve worked to get things back to normal after the military transport you were piloting took on enemy fire and crashed into the side of a mountain in the middle of God-knows-where-a-stan. That’s what the Army called it when they telephoned Mom and Dad at three o’clock in the morning, anyway.”

As if in response to the mention of the incident, Quinn’s left ankle came to life with a burning ache that she had begun to become accustomed to.

Quinn sighed, but said nothing. She pushed up the lever on the side of the steering column, signaling a turn, and then guided the sedan off the state highway and onto the interstate.

"I'm fine." She spoke quietly, not really sure if she believed those words. From the look on her sister's face, the younger woman certainly didn't.

"Mom said you've stopped going to physical therapy."

Oh, goddamn.

"What part of 'I'm fine' is not clear? Can we not talk about this? Don't you have a presentation you should be going over or something?"

"Nope, I'm all ready to go, thank you. I know you don't want to talk about this, but you've been avoiding the subject for too long now. Erin said you won't even take her calls anymore. We have at least another half hour before we get to Marietta, so unless you're planning on throwing me out of the car…"

"Now there's an idea," Quinn muttered, making sure she said it loud enough for her sister to hear.

"…which you are not going to do," Rebekah continued, "then you can be quiet and listen to what I have to say."

Quinn pursed her lips, remaining silent. Quinn wasn't going to give her younger sister – her younger, notoriously flaky sister – the satisfaction of knowing that her words were hitting home. She could tell from the look on her sister's face that she was getting some small measure of enjoyment out of being the one in control of the conversation. It occurred to her that Rebekah sounded more like their older sister Erin than the younger woman's usual scattered, slightly neurotic self. Quinn wondered if everyone else that Rebekah knew really was too busy to take her to the meeting today, or if this was some sort of twisted intervention scheme her sisters had dreamed up.

"First of all, let me say that Laurie was a bitch."

"What?" Quinn said, tapping the brake pedal.

"You heard me. You tried to make it work. Any kind of hang-up that woman had over your accident is completely on her and has nothing to do with you."

Goddamn it, this is an intervention.

"Rebekah…" Quinn began in a threatening tone.

"Nope, I'm the one doing the talking here. It's been how long? Six months? Seven months since the bitch walked out? And why? Because she's a superficial bitch."

"Know any words other than bitch?" Quinn mumbled off-handedly.

"How 'bout skank?"

Quinn couldn't help but give a little laugh. "Skank? Really Rebekah?"

"Yes, skank. What else would you call someone who breaks up a relationship because she *can't handle* looking at your scars?" Quinn began to chew on her bottom lip, but said nothing as her sister continued her rant. "I mean, what the fuck? They're your goddamned scars. You were the one that had to go through that hell and are still going through hell, no matter what you say. So, yes, she is a skank and she is not worth pining over."

"I'm not pining over anyone," Quinn said.

"Do you still have that cat that she left at your house when she packed up and moved out six months ago?"

Quinn cut her eyes over to her sister, but didn't respond.

"Exactly. She's a bitch and you need to get over it and on with your life. Just because she had a problem with it, doesn't mean anyone else will. And if they do, they're not worth your time anyway."

"Yes, mom."

"Whatever," Rebekah said, shaking her head with a smile. "Not like you were anything to look at in the first place."

"What?" Quinn turned her head sharply towards her sister, not sure she had just heard her correctly.

"We all know who got the looks in the family," Rebekah replied, opening the mirror on the visor to fluff her hair.

"You are unbelievable."

"That's what they say, isn't it? I get it all the time," the younger woman said, grinning.

"Whatever," Quinn said smiling. "Here's the exit. McDonald's sound okay? Or do you want to find a sit down place? We still have plenty of time."

"McDonald's sounds fine to me."

"Okay, great."

As Quinn pulled the sedan off the interstate and onto the exit ramp, her sister began to talk about her line and what she planned to say to the owners of the boutique. Quinn half-listened as Rebekah droned on about clutches and totes and bracelets, instead thinking about what her sister had said. Sometimes, despite all odds, the scatterbrain actually made sense.

Chapter Two

It was going to be a long day. Alison Jenkins walked through the small boutique that sat on the north end of the Square in downtown Marietta with the thought running through her head, not for the first time that morning.

An eclectic collection of restaurants, boutiques, antique shops, and theatres, the Square was the heart of the old town. Allie had always thought of it as a sort of oasis from the hustle and bustle of Atlanta and its busy suburbs. When the opportunity arose to invest with her cousin Amanda in opening a boutique on the Square four years ago, she jumped at it. Specializing in what Allie liked to call Southern Chic, Mimi's was not only one of the most successful shops on the square, but one of five that she and her cousin now owned in the greater Atlanta area.

Allie no longer handled the day to day operations of the stores, they had managers for that, but she and Amanda still acted as primary buyers for the chain of stores. One of the things that made their stores unique was that they specialized in apparel and products designed and produced in the Southeast. Which was the reason she was up and at the main store at eight o'clock in the morning on a Saturday.

Allie glanced at the small red clock that hung over the doorway.

God, is it really only eight-fifteen?

She had set the appointment to meet with a new designer for nine that morning. Allie had thought that would give her plenty of time to drive to the shop, stop along the way to get her morning infusion of coffee and do a quick inventory check at the store when she arrived. She hadn't counted on there being seemingly no traffic whatsoever on I-75, or that she would be the first customer through the door at the little coffee shop on the other side of the Square. As a result, she now had all the time in the world before the appointment. She could have slept in another forty-five minutes.

Allie wandered through the shop, absently straightening items here and there as she went. As she was considering killing some time by walking back over to the coffee shop for a second cup of hazelnut latte, Allie observed two women walk up and stop by the boutique's plate glass front door.

Both women were of similar height and had the same shade of honey-auburn hair, although the one holding a large cardboard box wore hers long and drawn back into a ponytail. What looked to be the older of the two had her hair cropped shorter, resting just at the shoulders. Thankful that the designer was early, Allie picked up the keys from beside the cash register and began walking over to unlock the front door. She couldn't help but notice the women embrace, the older woman seeming to whisper something to the younger before lightly kissing her on the cheek and then stepping off the sidewalk in the direction of Glover Park.

Allie swung open the door with a smile and beckoned the young woman in.

"Good morning. You must be Rebekah Briscoe?"

"I am, thank you," she said, walking into the store. Allie noticed that she seemed to be having a hard time carrying the oversized box.

"Please, put that down before you kill yourself," she said, motioning to a spot just in front of the cash register.

"Thanks, it is getting to be a little heavy."

"Of course. I'm Allie by the way. I believe you've been speaking with my associate Amanda on the phone. She would be here today, but her youngest has t-ball practice."

"It's very nice to meet you Allie," Rebekah said with a smile. Allie could tell that the young woman was doing her best not to look nervous, but her fidgeting feet and constant wiping of palms on her jeans gave her away.

"I know this is a business meeting, but it's really chilly outside this morning. I really don't mind if you want to ask your girlfriend to come inside while we go over everything,"

Allie said, thinking to make the young woman feel more at ease.

Rebekah looked at her, raised an eyebrow, and cocked her head.

"My girlfriend?"

Allie nodded and motioned towards the door.

"The other woman outside. I'm sorry, I saw her giving you a kiss and I guess I just assumed that she was your partner or girlfriend or something."

"Oh, Lord no," Rebekah said, barking out a laugh. "She is most definitely not my girlfriend. I am very much into men, thank you."

It was Allie's turn to raise an eyebrow. *Really?* Allie realized she must have *the look*, the one that said 'did I really just really hear you say that' on her face, because Rebekah suddenly paled and threw her hands up in the air.

"Oh no, I didn't mean it that way."

"No, it's okay," Allie said humorlessly. "Like I said, it was forward of me to make any assumptions."

"No, really. You don't understand. I don't have problems with gay people."

"Well, I'm very happy to hear that."

"Shit. I mean…I'm sorry, I didn't mean to say that. I mean, I didn't mean to say shit, not that I don't have problems with gay people. Because I don't."

"Don't worry about it," Allie said flatly. Damn, but she was going to hell for enjoying the young woman's obvious distress as much as she was.

"Oh my God, really. I don't want you to think I'm some sort of homophobe or something, because I'm not. I love lesbians. Well, I don't *love* lesbians because I'm into guys, but if that is your thing then I'm totally okay with it, really I am."

"Well, that's a relief."

Rebekah looked like she was about throw up.

"No. Oh my God. I'm babbling like an idiot, I know. But seriously, I know a lot of lesbians."

"You do?"

"Fuck me, now I sound like Archie Bunker."

Straight to hell, Allie thought.

"Do you want to start this over?" she asked the young woman, walking over and leaning against the check-out counter.

Rebekah's eyes got wide as she nodded vigorously.

"Oh my God, yes please. Thank you. Please, hold on one second," she said and then turned and ran out of the store.

Allie watched the plate glass door close and then said aloud to the empty store, “Well, that was interesting.”

When Rebekah didn’t return within a couple of minutes, Allie decided to inspect the contents of the cardboard box while she waited. She bent down and opened the box and then pulled out a colorful, hand-stitched tote. She turned it over in her hands, admiring the handiwork.

Very nice.

The sound of voices drew her attention away from the tote. Rebekah and the other woman stood by the front door, Rebekah pulling on her friend’s arm. For her part, the older woman did not look happy.

“Jesus, Rebekah, you weren’t in there ten minutes. How could you have fucked it up that bad in so short a time?”

“Seriously Quinn, now is not the time.”

Allie grinned and held back the urge to laugh at the exchange. She placed the tote back into the box and straightened up.

“Hello again,” she said, smiling at the two women as they entered the store. Allie saw now that she had a closer look at the other woman—Quinn, apparently—that this was obviously Rebekah’s sister. Though slightly taller, Quinn bore a striking resemblance to Rebekah. Both women had the same general facial structure, but there were differences that

Allie couldn't help but notice. While they both had blue eyes, the older woman's were a deeper shade. And there was something about her nose…

"Allie, this is my sister Quinn," Rebekah announced breathlessly. Evidently she had had to run across the park to retrieve her sister.

"Hello, Quinn," Allie said. The other woman gave a faint smile and flashed a hand up in the air.

Broken, Allie thought suddenly. That's what it was. Quinn's nose had a slight crook in it as if it had been broken at some point in the past. Not something you see every day, especially on a woman as attractive as Quinn.

"She's a lesbian," Rebekah blurted. Quinn snapped her head in her sister's direction at the outburst.

"Oh goddamn, Rebekah," she said sharply. "Have you lost your mind?"

Allie couldn't help but laugh. Hard. She leaned back against the counter for support and began to wipe her eyes. She looked up to see both sisters staring at her. She flashed back a grin and suddenly found her eyes drawn to an odd mark on the left side of Quinn's face. It took a second to register what it was. A scar. The raised pink flesh stood out in deep contrast against her pale complexion and ran a jagged line from the edge of Quinn's jawline down to her neck, disappearing beneath the white collar of her polo shirt.

Allie realized that she was staring at the same moment she realized that Quinn was staring back. She flushed with embarrassment and any hope she had that the older Briscoe sister had not noticed her transgression was dashed when she saw the woman's dark blue eyes turn to midnight.

Damn.

"So…" Allie began, needing to change the subject, "…like I said earlier, would you like to start over?" She reached down and picked up the tote again. "I was looking at this while you were gone, and I'm very impressed with the craftsmanship. What can you tell me about it?"

Rebekah beamed and leapt forward, grabbing the tote from Allie's hand and launching into detail about its construction. Rebekah then reached in the box and pulled out a clutch and began to sing its praises. Allie smiled and engaged the young woman in conversation about the purses and the prospect for sales at her stores. She stole a guilty glance at Rebekah's sister and found the woman glaring back at her sullenly.

Really, really long day…

Falling Slowly

Chapter Three

There was a blinding flash of light followed almost immediately by a loud clunk and an abrupt odor of sulfur. As the world suddenly turned sideways, Quinn felt her stomach lurch up towards her throat and threaten to bring the stale bagel that had been breakfast with it.

"What the hell?" A man's voice shouted directly into Quinn's ears through her headset. She looked to her side to see CW3 Tom Sullivan—Sully as he was called around post—pulling back sharply on the stick as the UH-60 yawed to the right.

"We're losing thrust," she answered back. "Hit the transponder." She reached up and pushed a button on the side of the headset. "Everybody hold on back there, it's fixing to be a rough ride."

The words had barely left her lips when another bright flash and then a sudden absence of sound.

The world returned in patches. There was an odd reverberating hum that seemed to echo in her head. A sharp thud. Clatter that made no sense.

It took a moment for Quinn to realize her eyes were closed. She was able to open one of them. The right didn't seem to be working, but that was okay as she was seeing two of everything with the other one. As the blurs slowly began to take shape into recognizable objects, she could hear a low keening sound coming from somewhere behind her.

Quinn reached down to release the seat harness, turning her head to the right as she did. Sully's lifeless face stared back at her, or at least what was left of it. The lower half of his jaw was disconnected from the rest of his face and hung loosely by a few strips of skin.

Quinn closed her eye and willed herself not to vomit.

"Motherfucker."

A man's voice broke through and she looked back up to see a soldier crawling up from the side of the helicopter. Her working eye flashed to his chest and she was startled to read the name affixed to his uniform jacket. Morales. The blackened, bloodied face that swam in front of hers now looked nothing like the tanned, smiling twenty-something with just a hint of five o'clock shadow that had boarded the helicopter barely an hour ago.

"Captain, you alive?" She nodded and was immediately sorry for the action. Pain shot through her neck and down into her chest.

"Sully," she croaked, motioning to the other side of the cockpit, surprised by the sound of her own voice.

The soldier shook his head.

“Naw, don’t look over there. You don’t need to see that.”

Too late, she thought. The acrid smell of charred electronics and burning flesh singed her nose, bringing Quinn out of her daze.

“We need to get out of here,” she said, pulling off the harness that held her in the seat. “It won’t take them long to be swarming all over us.”

Morales nodded as he pressed a hand firmly to the side of her neck. “Let’s get on it then, but you’re bleeding like a stuck pig. If we don’t do something about it soon…” His voice trailed off.

“Look behind the seat. There’s a first aid kit in the back.” Quinn motioned over her head with one hand and covered the wound with the other. She tried to ignore the sickening warmth that seeped through her fingers, dripping onto the shoulder of her uniform. As Morales moved to the rear of the seat, she began to rise. The motion caused her world to explode in white hot agony.

“Oh goddamn!” she cried and drew in a sharp breath, pushing back the darkness that began to swim around her.

Morales materialized in front of her. “Captain?”

“My leg,” she rasped. Tears welled up in her eyes as boiling currents of pain swept up from her left leg.

Morales frowned and then knelt in front of her to inspect the damage. She heard him suck in a breath as he pulled back on the fabric of her pant leg.

"Titty fucking Christ!" he exclaimed and then immediately shot a worried glance up at her. "I'm sorry, Captain. I didn't mean no disrespect."

"Sergeant, are you kidding me? I think that's the least of our worries right now, don't you?"

He laughed and nodded his head. "I guess you're right. This is bad. You got some kinda…I don't know what it is. Like a bar. It's bent across your leg sideways. Well, bent into your leg. Damn, that's gotta hurt."

"Can you bend it back the other way?" she asked between clenched teeth.

"Lemme try."

Quinn closed her eye again and braced for the pain that she knew would be coming. She felt him lay a firm hand on the top of her boot and then grunt as he pulled on the metal. It felt like fire erupting from her leg and she tried to bite back a scream. At that moment she would have welcomed unconsciousness, but it failed to come.

"Here it comes…Motherfucker!" she finally heard him say and then the unbearable pressure was gone. A fiery ache continued to smolder along the length of her leg, but it paled in comparison to the former.

"Oh, God," she moaned and then took a deep breath. "We gotta get going, Sergeant. I'd rather not become some Taliban's good time tonight."

Morales flashed a grin at her, his teeth white against his smoke-blackened face. "You and me both, Captain. Here, let me get our shit together and then I'll be back to carry you." As Quinn sat up and started to protest, he shook his head. "Be real. Ain't no way you're going to be able walk on that leg. And you're bleeding all over."

Quinn nodded and laid her head back against the seat. A thought suddenly occurred to her.

"Wait a minute," she said. "Where's the rest of your team?"

Morales' eyes darkened and he shook his head. She grimaced and nodded, trying not to think about the four dead men in the back of the helicopter—or the one sitting next to her—as she held a hand to the gash along her neck. As quickly as he was gone, Morales returned, wearing a large camouflage backpack and a pair of rifles slung over one shoulder.

"Okay, let's get moving," he said as he reached out and lifted her from the cockpit. The movement ignited the fire in her leg again and she gasped, retching and spitting up the bile that had been threatening since the crash. Morales grunted and shifted her in his arms. It was all too much and she gave in to the blackness that called her.

Beep-Beep-Beep-Beep.

Quinn gasped and sat up in her bed as the shrill sound of her alarm cut through the room, waking her from the dream…from her nightmare. With a quick swipe she silenced the alarm. She shivered and lay back on the bed, curling over on her side, wrapping the heavy comforter tightly around her as she did. Quinn closed her eyes and willed away the memories that haunted her dreams. It'd been a long time since she'd had a dream as vivid as that one, and she wondered what had triggered it.

Rebekah and her intervention shit.

Since the day of the meeting at that boutique in Marietta, Rebekah had made herself a constant fixture in Quinn's life, whether Quinn wanted it or not. Despite her reluctance to go on the forced shopping excursions, outings to local restaurants for lunch and dinner, and even an overnight jaunt up to North Carolina for a trip to the Cherokee casino, Quinn had to admit she was feeling better. Both about herself and just better in general.

Not that she would admit that to her younger sister.

After a few minutes of semi-snooze, Quinn groaned and rolled over on her back. If she didn't get up now she was going to be late for physical therapy. Another thing that Rebekah and the rest of the family fancied themselves responsible for.

Quinn tossed back the comforter and swung her legs off the bed, swallowing as a faint burning pain tickled around her neck and down her leg, a ghost from the dream world. As she rose from the bed she caught a glimpse of the calico cat leisurely making its way to her pillow and settling down in the center of it.

"I really can't stand you, cat," Quinn called out as she made her way out of the bedroom.

Chapter Four

Allie wrinkled her nose as the acrid smell of burnt popcorn wafted from the concession area over to the cold metal bleachers where she sat. She frowned and tossed a glare in the direction of the small, yellow brick building that sat at the northern end of Liam Park. A line of children edged around the side, laughing and chattering as they waited.

"Lord, is there anything worse than the smell of burnt popcorn?"

Her cousin Amanda looked up from the iPad resting on her knee, shook her head, then pushed a fallen strand of blonde hair back behind one ear.

"Doubt it. You'd think it wouldn't be that hard to make popcorn. But then again, we are talking about teenagers making like eight dollars an hour, so I guess we're lucky they don't burn the place down."

"Tell me about it," Allie remarked. "Oh, there's Nicky. He looks so cute in his little uniform." She motioned to the baseball field in front of them, where a diminutive little boy in a bright blue shirt and gray baseball pants was making his way out from the dugout to home plate.

Amanda smiled and waved at her son as he looked up into the stands at her.

"He does, doesn't he?" She settled in to watch his at-bat. Shivering, she drew up a small green blanket sitting beside her on the bleacher and wrapped it around her arms. "Why they have to play so early in the morning is beyond me."

"It is a little chilly, isn't it?" Allie said, rubbing a hand over one arm.

"You should have stayed home where it's warm. I *have* to be here, no reason for both of us to catch our death from pneumonia."

"Please, like I would miss a single game of the Greater Cobb County Professional T-Ball League. Chipper Jones has nothing on Nicky Nolan," she grinned.

Amanda shook her head. "Please, I should be so lucky. Wouldn't break my heart to have Nicky go pro and bring home the millions. You know little boys love their mothers and always make sure they are taken care of."

"Oh, whatever."

"You'll see one day."

"Mmmhmm, well is that little Chipper there running the wrong way after hitting the ball?" Allie asked, laughing as Nicky barreled his way from home to third base.

Amanda covered her eyes and groaned.

"Well, maybe we have a few more years before the big leagues come calling."

"Poor baby, he's trying." Allie stood up and clapped as Nicky, having been tagged out at third, glumly made his way back to the dugout. "Good effort Nicky, good effort!" she called out.

Amanda turned her attention back to the iPad and began to absently swipe at the screen. After a moment, she glanced at Allie and said, "So…speaking of one day…"

"One day what?" Allie asked, cocking an eyebrow.

"Well, you're not getting any younger, to channel Grandma Jenkins for just a moment. Any new prospects that I should know about?"

"Really, Amanda? Don't you have anything better to gossip about than my love life?

"Apparently you don't, or you wouldn't be spending a Saturday morning out watching other people's children play t-ball. Even if one of them does belong to your favorite first cousin."

"My only first cousin…"

"Minor detail," Amanda snipped. "Seriously, though. There's got to be some cute little girl just waiting for you out there."

Allie snorted and shook her head. "Okay, now you're making me sound like a pedophile." She reached and picked up a plastic Diet Coke bottle sitting to her right.

"Woman, then. Although…"

"Although what?" she asked, taking a sip of the soda.

Amanda looked up from the iPad and smirked at Allie. "Maybe you can go trolling around Kennesaw State and pick you up a hot, young college girl. Surely somebody out there is looking for a Sugar Mama?"

"Well, you've lost your mind, haven't you?"

Amanda laughed. "Just sayin'. You should keep your options open."

"I think we can safely take that option off the table."

Amanda crossed her arms. "Okay, then. What options can we put on the table? How about that cute little insurance agent over on Depot Street? The one who walks around the park at lunch?"

Allie twisted her lips and shook her head. "Meh, she's a little too perky for my tastes."

"Okay then. The assistant manager at the Druid Hills store? I understand she's single again."

"Nope. Employees are definitely off the table. Besides, she strikes me as more bi-curious than anything."

"Bi-curious, hmm? Well, maybe you can swing her over to the dark side," Amanda said with a chuckle and then ducked as Allie tossed the half-empty soda bottle at her.

"Get off it, Amanda. Again…don't you have anything better to talk about than my love life?"

"Or lack thereof…" Amanda murmured, not quite under her breath.

Allie sighed and rolled her eyes. She motioned to the field. "Your child is waving at you, by the way."

Amanda looked up and out to left field, then waved to Nicky. She watched as he began to twirl around on one foot and look up at the sky, oblivious to the t-ball game going on around him. She shook her head and sighed. "Lord, he's never going to be Chipper Jones, is he?"

"I think the safe bet there would be no."

"Oh, well," she said and glanced back down at the iPad. "Oh," she said suddenly and looked back over to Allie. "I forgot to tell you. Those purses from that new girl from up in Pickens County have been a huge hit. Melanie said they can't keep them on the shelf in Buckhead, and they've got a waiting list for them at the Brookhaven store."

"Really? That's fantastic. I knew they would sell well. She seemed like a nice girl. A little off, but a nice girl."

Amanda frowned. "What do you mean *a little off*?"

"Nothing, really," Allie said, shaking her head and smiling.

"What?"

“Okay. It wasn’t anything, really. When she got to the store, I saw her kiss and hug another woman through the window before she came in. Naturally, I assumed—”

“That she was gay,” Amanda interjected. Allie nodded.

“So, when I very casually mentioned something about it—”

“She wasn’t,” Amanda interrupted again.

“Yes. But she told me *very emphatically* that she wasn’t—”

“And then you got mad and gave her that one-eyed look you give to people when they piss you off.”

“I don’t have a look, and certainly not a ‘one-eyed’ one.”

“You have a look.”

“Okay, I have a look, but I don’t know about one-eyed.”

Amanda shook her head. “Honey, I have known you longer than anyone and you have an evil little squinty one-eyed look.” As Allie scowled, she continued. “You do! You really need to watch what you say to people sometimes. I know that people in and around Atlanta live in the modern world, but there’s a whole lotta Georgia that doesn’t. I’m surprised that you agreed to take in her work. I know how you feel about homophobes.”

Allie rolled her eyes and snorted.

"Please, those people can watch out for *me*. I am quite comfortable with who I am, thank you very much. Besides, she didn't fall into that category."

"Oh?"

"No. Like I said, she was nice, just a little off. She was so nervous she almost made me shake, to tell you the truth." Allie pointed to the field again. "Look, Nicky is making sandcastles out there in the dirt."

"What? Oh Lord, Nicky!" Nicky's head perked up from the red sand that surrounded left field. "Stop that!" Amanda called out to him.

Allie covered her mouth and all but cackled.

"Yeah, I don't think you have to worry about the big leagues calling anytime soon," she laughed as her cousin sat back down on the bleacher.

"Lord," Amanda muttered. She shook her head and then turned back to Allie. "So who was the woman?"

"What?"

"The girl. Rebekah Whatsername. You said she was hugging some woman outside the store. So, who was she?"

"Oh. It was just her sister. She had driven her down to the shop."

"Better sister than I would be to get up that early on a Saturday," Amanda remarked and watched, relieved, as Nicky's team headed back to the dugout.

"Briscoe."

"What?"

"That's her last name. Briscoe." Allie had a fleeting image of the girl's attractive sister. *Very attractive sister.* "And I believe Quinn was her sister's name."

"Hmmphf."

Allie turned at the sound and stared at her cousin.

"What do you mean *hmmphf*?"

The other woman gave a sly smile. "I think you know what I mean. I heard the way you said the sister's name."

"Oh?" Allie asked, raising one eyebrow. "And what way did I say it?"

"You know."

"I'm sure I don't," Allie said.

"I'm sure you do. *Quinn.*"

"Oh, please."

"I know you better than you know yourself Alison Jenkins. Let me guess. Was she hot?"

"You really need to get a new hobby."

"No wait…" Amanda's eyes narrowed. "Was she a hot lesbian?" Allie ignored her, turning her focus instead to the team of six-year-olds taking the field. Amanda snapped, causing Allie to jump. “I knew it! You have been keeping something from me.”

Allie exhaled noisily.

“I think we’ve established already that you’ve lost your mind.”

“I think we’ve established that there *is* a prospect out there. If she’s hot, why haven’t you gone for that, Miss ‘I’m comfortable with who I am’?” Amanda crossed her arms and looked sharply at Allie.

“Not going to happen. Let’s just say I did not make a good first impression.”

“Well, then,” Amanda said, licking her lips. “I think it’s time we arranged a second impression.”

Chapter Five

"I can't believe I let you talk me into this."

"Oh, Quinn."

"Don't 'Oh, Quinn' me. You're going to owe me for this one."

Quinn eased back on the hunter green couch that sat in the corner of her living room, left leg crossed over her right, absently massaging her ankle with one hand. She'd been watching her sister Rebekah flutter around the house for the past couple of hours. Fluffing and re-fluffing pillows, straightening pictures on the wall that didn't need straightening. Quinn was fairly certain that she had swept the kitchen at least twice. She knew for a fact that Rebekah had cleaned the litter box that sat in the guest bathroom three times. Every time she scooped it out, the cat walked back in behind her to make another deposit. Rebekah had positioned scented candles all over the house. The strange combination of scents—apple spice, gingerbread, gardenia, and lemon—bit at Quinn's nose and was beginning to give her a headache.

"Whatever," Rebekah said, glancing out the kitchen window. "It's not like you were going to do anything today anyway."

"Remind me again why I keep helping you?" Quinn asked with a slight scowl.

Rebekah walked back into the living room and began to rearrange the trinkets on a bookshelf that sat beside a large bay window. "Because you love me," she said sweetly.

Like a hole in my head.

"I still don't know why you couldn't meet with these people at your own house," Quinn said, grinning as she noticed the calico cat leisurely walk out of the bedroom and head towards the guest bathroom.

"You know my place is not that big. Erin's has always got kids and animals running through it," she said, turning to look at Quinn. "And there's no way in hell I would even think about Mom and Dad's house."

Quinn barked out a laugh and shook her head at that image. "Would serve that rude bitch right to have to go there. I can see Mom now trying to force feed her chocolate chip cookies while extolling your virtues endlessly."

"Well, at least someone likes to extoll them, as you say." Rebekah crossed her arms and leaned back against the bookshelf. "And stop calling her a rude bitch. She was very nice that day we met her. Besides, that rude bitch has made me a butt-load of money over the past month or so."

"A butt-load, huh? Do I even want to know how much that is?" Quinn smirked.

"Enough to finally get my car fixed," Rebekah answered.

"Well, thank God for that." Quinn turned on the couch, propping her head on a pillow and stretching out her legs. "And she *was* a rude bitch, by the way."

"Please, you just got upset because you caught her looking…"

"Staring," Quinn interjected sharply.

"Okay, *staring* at your neck. But, you know how people are. Especially around Atlanta, where they have no manners whatsoever. Just because that skank Laurie…"

"Oh Lord, are we back on her again?" Quinn mumbled, closing her eyes.

"Yes, we are. Just because the skank said the things she did, doesn't mean everyone is like that. People can be curious without being repulsed, Quinn."

"Well, people can mind their own damn business."

Rebekah gave a short laugh. "Just wait 'til summer rolls around. Eventually you're going to have to get out of those jeans and put on a pair of shorts. Won't that be a show?" Rebekah squeaked and quickly dodged the pillow that Quinn threw across the room at her. "You gotta stop worrying about what people are gonna think or say."

"Whatever," Quinn muttered, aggravated both at her sister and the fact that she knew most of what Rebekah was saying was true. She'd never been overly concerned about her looks or really self-conscious in any way. *Well, at least not before*. "So, what time are they supposed to be here?"

"Soon. Amanda said on the phone that she and Allie wanted to check out the downtown area and see if there were any viable spaces for a store. All those Atlanta folks moving up to that area around Lake Tamarack, they think that there is market potential in Pickens County."

Quinn laughed and sat up on the couch. "Ha! Market potential. Aren't you little Miss Business all of a sudden?" Even as she said the words, Quinn was proud of her sister. Her line of designer purses was selling off the shelves at the boutiques in the Metro Atlanta area and for once something her sister was doing seemed to be paying off.

"Bite me," Rebekah snapped back at her. "Amanda said that after they got through up that way, they would stop by on the way back home to say hello and talk shop."

Quinn stretched and then stood, yawning as she walked towards the kitchen.

"Well, try not to talk all night. That little guy just about killed me at PT today. I'm sore in places I didn't know I had. I'm ready to get them—and you—out of here and get settled in for the evening." Quinn opened the refrigerator door and reached in to pull out a drink. "Want a Coke or something?" she called out to her sister.

"No, I'm fine," Rebekah said, shaking her head. "I think I'll just—are you kidding me! Damn it Quinn, that shitting-ass cat of yours is at it again in the litter box!"

Quinn burst out laughing as she could hear the tell-tale sound of a paw scratching at sand coming from the bathroom.

"Serves you right," she said. "You've got it smelling like a fucking Afghan bazaar up in here with all those damn candles. He's probably just trying to get rid of the god-awful smell *you've* created."

Quinn laughed again as she heard her sister begin to rant and chase after the cat. She walked across the kitchen and then stopped, glancing out the window over the sink.

"I'd forget about the cat if I were you. They're here."

"What?" Rebekah cried out and ran into the kitchen. "Of all times, damn it. God, I hate your cat."

"Join the club," Quinn muttered as she watched the doors of a black Jeep Grand Cherokee open and the two women step out. Rude Bitch exited the driver's door and walked to the front of the vehicle before stopping. She looked back as the other woman, a plump thirty-something with bright blonde hair whom Quinn assumed was Amanda, walked around to the back of the vehicle and opened the hatch.

Quinn grinned wryly as she noticed Rude Bitch pull a bright pink compact out of her purse and seem to check her hair and make-up. Not that either were out of place, she noted. The woman's long, golden brown hair seemed perfect as it framed her face, nicely complimenting her pink, full lips. There was a time, Quinn reflected silently, that she could see herself becoming enchanted with lips like that.

"Quinn, please don't embarrass me," Rebekah said from the doorway of the kitchen, interrupting her thoughts. "And can you please do something about the cat?"

She tossed a sideways glance at Rebekah and sighed, shaking her head as she walked away from the window.

Chapter Six

"Now look, Allie," Amanda said, walking around the side of the Jeep. "You've already fucked up the first go round with this chick, so don't screw this up."

Allie dropped the pink compact back into the purse and lowered her eyes at Amanda.

"I still can't believe I let you talk me into this," she said in a low voice as they stepped away from the vehicle, glancing up at the grey, Craftsman-style house with black shutters along the front. The small front yard was kept neat, with a smattering of flowering bushes that ran the length of the front porch. "There are plenty of so-called prospects around that we don't have to skulk up here in some kind of warped scheme to find me a date."

Amanda made a noise. "That may be, but you have not shown the slightest bit of interest in any of them. It won't kill you to just see what happens." She stopped on the bottom porch step and turned back to face Allie. "Besides," she said, placing a hand on one hip, "we want to keep these girls happy. I'd hate for Hot Chick to talk her sister into pulling her line from the stores because you don't know how to act in front of people."

“What the hell is that supposed to mean?” Allie asked sharply.

“Just what I said.” With that, Amanda continued up the stairs and tapped lightly on the front door. After only a moment, the door swung open and Rebekah’s smiling face greeted them.

“Hi, come on in,” she beamed at the two women and stepped to one side, motioning for Amanda and Allie to follow her. “I hope you didn’t have any problems finding the place.”

“No, not at all,” Amanda answered. “We came right to it. It really didn’t take as long as I thought it might, to tell you the truth.”

At least that was true, Allie thought to herself as she followed behind Amanda through the foyer and into what looked to be the living room. They had spent most of the morning in the small, upscale community an hour north of Atlanta shopping and gauging whether there would be enough market potential to consider opening a store in the downtown area.

“What did you think of Lake Tamarack?” Rebekah asked.

"It was—" Amanda suddenly stopped so abruptly that Allie would have ran into her had she not been paying attention. Her cousin made an odd, retching sort of noise.

What the hell?

A moment later it hit Allie like a punch in the face. She felt a surge jump up her throat from her stomach and closed her eyes, willing herself not to vomit.

"Oh my Jesus," she croaked and covered her face with one hand, trying not to inhale. For just a moment her mind stopped working as it tried to process the origin of what had to be the single most horrific smell she had ever encountered.

"Goddamn it, Rebekah, I told you those candles were going to kill somebody."

She blinked back tears to see Rebekah's sister storm into the living room, throw back curtains and open the large bay window on the near side of the room. Allie gave a slight cough as Rebekah grabbed her sister by one arm and pulled her into the kitchen. Allie and Amanda exchanged glances as they heard the muffled sound of an argument between the two women.

What the hell has Amanda got me into?

Rebekah walked quickly back into the living room.

"God, I am so sorry. I didn't realize the smell was that strong," she apologized.

“What is that?” Amanda asked with a bit of wheeze in her voice.

“Rebekah blew up a Yankee Candle factory in here just before you arrived. She was afraid you’d smell the cat box in the other room,” Quinn said. Allie realized that she’d never really heard the woman speak before. The woman with the honey-auburn hair had a husky tone to her voice, almost sultry.

“That’s what that is,” she heard Amanda say. “I can smell it now. It’s like…fruity cat shit.”

Allie jumped slightly as Rebekah’s sister barked out a laugh, catching her by surprise.

“With just a touch of gingerbread,” Quinn added smiling. “Please, come on in. Hopefully that smell will go away here in a just a bit. Make yourselves comfortable.”

“Thank you,” Allie said, still not quite sure as she sat tentatively next to Amanda on the edge of a dark green couch. Rebekah took a seat opposite them on a high back chair of the same color. Quinn, Allie noted, remained standing. She leaned against the large doorway that separated the living room from the kitchen area, arms crossed, a not quite smile on her face as she appeared to study Allie and Amanda.

"So, Rebekah says you ladies drove up to Lake Tamarack today."

"We did," Amanda said. "It was gorgeous scenery, but I'm not sure if it's going to be right for us. It may be a little too out of the way."

"Not quite downtown Atlanta, is it?"

"No," Allie added, "but I'm not sure that's necessarily a bad thing."

Quinn simply nodded. It occurred to Allie that she seemed to be sizing them up. Probably trying to look out for her sister. What was it that Grandma Jenkins used to say? Trying to gauge whether they were 'good people' or not.

"Can I get you something to drink?" Quinn finally said, breaking the awkward silence. "Coke, Diet Coke, coffee, water?"

"A Diet Coke would be just fine," Allie answered.

"Make that two," Amanda said.

"Of course," Quinn said with a nod and turned, heading back through the doorway into the kitchen. For the first time, Allie noticed that the slender woman had a very pronounced limp as she watched her shuffle out of the room. Allie suddenly felt a sharp jab in her side and looked to see Amanda scowling at her.

Oh God, I was staring again.

“So…” Allie began, looking across the room at Rebekah, anxious to turn the subject. “I’m sure Amanda told you how well your line has been selling at the stores.”

The young woman smiled broadly and nodded her head. “She did. It’s just so thrilling to be able to see people love my designs as much as I do.”

“Well, you’re very talented,” Quinn said, walking back into the room with a glass in each hand, offering the drinks to Allie and Amanda. “As I’m sure Amanda and her associate are well aware.” Allie noted that Rebekah looked at her sister and gave her an odd look as she spoke.

“Thank you,” Allie said quietly, noting the use of ‘associate’ rather than her name. She thought that she had left a bad impression with Quinn the day they met at the boutique and now she was sure of it.

“There are coasters on the side table there,” Quinn advised. Allie smiled and turned to her left in search of one for Amanda and herself. As she reached to pick two of the coasters up from a small, wrought iron stand, her eyes were suddenly drawn to a picture frame sitting beside it.

“Oh my goodness, is that you?” she asked, motioning to the photo of what looked to be a slightly younger, much friendlier looking Quinn standing with a group of soldiers in front of a very large, black helicopter.

"It is," Rebekah answered for her sister. "Quinn used to fly Black Hawks when she was in the Army."

"Technically, I'm still in the Army, Rebekah," Allie heard Quinn murmur to her sister as she took in more details of the picture. Quinn, along with the men in the photo, wore a tan-green uniform and had a helmet perched under one arm. They looked to be standing on a runway of sorts, and Allie could just make out dark colored mountains in the background. She thought about the scar along Quinn's neck. *So, that explains that.*

"That explains what?" a gravelly voice said sharply behind her. Allie felt her stomach drop and she looked up to see Quinn narrow her eyes into a glare. *Tell me I didn't say that out loud.*

"Your little helicopter collection over there," Amanda quickly interjected, motioning to the bookshelf by the window. "I noticed that myself when we arrived. Not something you see every day, but I suppose it makes sense if you're a pilot."

Quinn glanced behind her at the row of miniature helicopters that lined one shelf. The moment she turned her head, Amanda kicked Allie in the shin.

"Seriously?" Amanda mouthed to her cousin, shaking her head.

Quinn looked back to the women and nodded, blue eyes flashing at Allie. "One of my nephews gave me those for Christmas last year," she said in a low voice and then excused herself from the room, stepping back into the kitchen.

"So, Rebekah, I brought you some of those samples we talked about on the phone. They're out in the car if you'd like to go see them," Amanda said with an overly bright smile.

"That would be wonderful," Rebekah answered, rising from the chair. Amanda stood and leaned over Allie.

"Damn it, Allie!" she whispered. "You have five minutes to go fix that."

Allie exhaled heavily as Amanda and Rebekah made their way towards the front door.

"Are you coming Allie?" Rebekah asked.

She shook her head, ignoring a glaring Amanda standing behind the young woman.

"No, you go ahead. I may be out in a minute." She watched as the women walked down the hallway, chattering lightly as they went. *Fix it, huh? Like I'm damn Bob the Builder.*

Allie heaved a sigh and then rose from the couch. She walked quietly into the kitchen to find Quinn head down, both hands resting against the sink.

“Quinn?” she said tentatively.

The other woman’s head snapped up and she turned sharply to look at Allie, her dark blue eyes flashing with undisguised animosity.

“Quinn, I feel like we got off on the wrong foot, and I want to apologize.”

“You do, huh?” The words were almost a sneer.

Allie swallowed before answering. “Yes. I know what happened the other morning at the store…well, happened. And I’m sorry if I made you feel uncomfortable. Then or just now. It was certainly not my intention.”

“Really?” Quinn crossed her arms and leaned back against the sink

“Yes, really. I’m not normally that kind of person, so I don’t want you to have the wrong impression.”

“And what impression would that be?” Quinn asked with more than a hint of hostility in her voice.

“That I—”

“That you’re a rude ass?” Quinn interrupted.

“What?” Allie felt a heat the in back of neck rise up. *I know she did not just say that.*

“You heard me. I’ve had more than…” Her voiced trailed away for a moment and then she breathed loudly. “…I’ve had it up to here with your kind, thank you very much. But you know, I don't even really care about that anymore. I'm just going to say one thing." Quinn took a step towards Allie. "My younger sister is happier than I've seen her in a long time. If you or your partner do anything to hurt her or try to take advantage of her in any way, then you'll have me to answer to."

Oh, hell no.

"Take advantage of her?" Allie asked, feeling her temper flare higher.

"You heard me."

"Well, you hear this. Don't *ever* accuse me—or my partner—of…what? Trying to cheat your sister out of something?"

"Exactly what I'm saying."

Allie felt her cheeks flush as the smoldering feeling of fury washed over her. She had worked too hard and made too many sacrifices over the past several years to not just make Mimi's a successful chain of stores, but one that had a reputation for treating both customers and designers fairly. To have this…this…woman stand here now and accuse her of being dishonest was outrageous.

"You rude ass bitch." As soon as the words left Quinn's lips, Allie's world took on a red tint.

"Oh, hell no. You can listen to me for a goddamn minute," Allie all but shouted, pointing a finger as she took her own step forward. "I might be a rude ass bitch for looking—no, you're right—staring at you. But you know what? Oh fucking well. Yeah, I was so shocked when I looked up in my own goddamn store and saw such a giant ugly ass scar on such a drop dead gorgeous woman that all I could do was stare."

"What did you just say?"

"You fucking heard me. But you know what? Get over it. I'm sorry that you got hit by a bomb or a MRE or whatever the fuck happened, but don't stand there and accuse me or my cousin of anything because you've got some kind of a giant chip on your shoulder. You can go fuck yourself."

Quinn opened her mouth to say something, but then closed it abruptly at the sound of the front door closing. She glanced over Allie's head towards the living room and the sound of Rebekah and Amanda coming back into the house, her nostrils flaring. She glared at Allie and then moved to leave the room, intentionally brushing past her. Quinn got to the doorway and then stopped. She stood there quietly for a minute and then turned on one heel to face Allie.

"IED," she said flatly.

Allie frowned and shook her head. "What?"

"It's not called a MRE, it's called an IED. MRE is…it's not the word you were looking for." With that, she turned and left the room, leaving Allie to stare after her.

"Allie," she heard Amanda call out. "How are things coming?"

Allie snorted and began to walk towards the living room to greet Amanda and Rebekah. Quinn was nowhere to be seen.

"Oh, I think things are pretty much done here."

Chapter Seven

Quinn reached over and unbuckled her seatbelt at the same time she turned the dark gray Toyota Camry off of North Avenue in Atlanta and into a parking space in front of the red and tan brick building that was The Varsity. She opened the car door and stepped out, sighing with contentment as she took in the aroma of hamburgers and fried grease that wafted outside the building.

The Varsity—specifically The Varsity's onion rings—was one of her few guilty pleasures. She had developed a taste for the deep fried, highly addictive circles of sinful goodness while a student at nearby Georgia Tech. While it wasn't often, Quinn made a point to stop by whenever she happened to find herself in the downtown Atlanta area to get a fix.

Quinn reached to open the heavy glass door with one hand and swiped off her uniform cap with the other, folding and sliding it into a side pocket on her digital camouflage pants. She'd spent most of the day at nearby Fort McPherson working on the paperwork that would complete her medical separation from the Army. *Medical retirement*, she thought, correcting herself. It seemed odd that at thirty-one she was going to be considered a retiree, but, with a forty percent disability rating due to the injuries she sustained in the crash, that was her new reality.

Choosing what looked to be the shortest line, Quinn fell in behind a young mother with one child on her hip and the other holding her hand. Quinn shifted uncomfortably in her brown suede boots as she waited, her left leg beginning to throb. It had been sometime since she had worn the boots all day and she was more than ready to get home and kick them off. Although she knew exactly what she was going to order, Quinn still looked absently at the menu board that hung on a wall behind the high checkout counter.

"What'll you have, what'll you have," a smiling elderly man in a white paper hat called out when she finally stepped up to the counter.

"Two naked dogs, an order of rings, and a large orange drink," she replied. She glanced back up at the board as she waited and briefly considered adding a fried peach pie to her order, then decided to wait and get it to go on her way out.

Quinn thanked the server as he slid the tray of food across the counter to her and then turned, trying to decide where she wanted to sit. She opted for one of the 'news' rooms, so designated by what channel the television set hanging on the wall was tuned to, thinking it should be relatively empty at this time of the day. She slid into the first empty booth and quietly arranged the food on the tray, moving the hot dogs to the side so that the onion rings took center stage.

She had just bitten into one of the deliciously hot rings when she picked up on a familiar voice from the far end of the room. She looked up, searching for and then finding the source. Quinn leveled her eyes on the back of Allie Jenkins' head as she slowly savored the onion ring.

What are the odds, she thought. It had been several weeks since the…whatever the hell that was…confrontation, maybe. She hadn't told Rebekah about the shouting match she'd had with the rude bitch because she didn't want to upset her. For her part, Rebekah was still doing very well on sales at the boutique. She seemed happy and spent most of her time working on and producing new designs for her line. They had already passed the typical timeframe in which Rebekah normally flaked out, so Quinn was hopeful that this particular endeavor would stay on course.

She continued to savor the food, listening to Allie's end of the cell phone conversation as she took a large bite of one of the hot dogs. The other woman, oblivious to Quinn's presence in the room, was having an argument with someone, or at least that was the impression Quinn got from the tone of Allie's voice.

Quinn had thought about the argument she'd had with Allie that day off and on over the past several weeks. She hadn't been talked to that way since the crash. People had a tendency to tip-toe around her and, with the exception of Rebekah who simply just didn't have a filter, guarded their words, always seeming to make sure they were politically correct when talking to her. Even friends she had known since high school made a specific point to *not* look at the jagged eight inch scar, so much so it was painfully obvious what they were not looking at. Few people seemed to be able to even utter the word 'scar' in her presence. She could only imagine what their reaction would be if they saw the mangled mess that was her left leg.

Probably think the same thing Laurie had, she reflected. Her ex-girlfriend had been supportive through that last deployment and in the aftermath of the crash. She'd made multiple visits to D.C. while Quinn was recovering at Walter Reed Medical Center for all those weeks. Once Quinn was back home, however, things seemed to change. Laurie stayed over at the house less and less, and reasons to cancel dates became more frequent. Sex was simply non-existent. Finally, after several months of skirting around the issue, Laurie finally came out and admitted that it was more than she could handle and left for a job in Birmingham. *Of course, she left that damn cat of hers with me.*

So, taking a large drink of orange soda, Quinn supposed it was almost a refreshing change to have someone point out that she, in fact, had a big ugly ass scar on the side of her neck. Of course, that that someone was an attractive woman with luscious pink lips who, in the same breath, had said that she thought Quinn was gorgeous certainly didn't hurt matters.

She had just finished off the last hot dog when she smelled—and then looked up to see—a large man in a ragged blue shirt all but stagger in the side door of the room. His hair was gunmetal gray and hung in pieces around his head. He reeked of body odor and urine, and didn't so much as walk as he did waddle. Quinn noticed track marks lined both arms, which were almost black with dirt and filth. The homeless were almost an epidemic throughout parts of the downtown area. Most had just had bad times go worse and tried to eke out an existence, going from shelter to shelter each night and living off the streets by day. Some, like the man lumbering towards the back corner where Allie was sitting, were heavy drug users and existed only to find a way to get money for their next hit.

Quinn saw Allie notice the man about the same time he reached her table. She saw Allie place the cell phone down and say something to the man quietly, shaking her head as she spoke. He scratched the side of his face and then moved in closer, pointing at something on her table.

Fuck, Quinn thought, rising up from her seat. She didn't particularly like the woman—or maybe she did. The stunningly attractive woman had certainly made more than one appearance in Quinn's dreams over the past few weeks. She didn't know what to think about Allie, but either way she couldn't leave her to fend for herself. Despite the attitude she had given Quinn the other day, Allie didn't come across as someone ready to handle a homeless junkie one on one.

Not that I am myself these days.

Quinn placed her drink back on the red plastic tray and then picked it up, carrying the tray with her as she made her way to the back corner booth. She quietly stepped up behind the two of them and hesitated for a moment. She still wasn't quite sure if she was going to intervene until she heard the slightest hint of a tremble in Allie's voice as she asked the man again to please go away.

"Is there something that I can help you with?" she said, frowning.

Both the man and Allie jumped and turned as she spoke. Quinn saw Allie look at her and then the woman's eyes go wide with recognition. From the look on her face, she couldn't help but wonder if Allie would have preferred the junkie's presence to her own.

Chapter Eight

"Is there something that I can help you with?"

The sound of the husky voice startled both Allie and the foul-smelling man, who had developed a keen interest in her iPhone. She glanced back in the direction of the speaker, careful not to take her hand off the phone. She squinted at the person, thankful for the interruption, and then was stunned to see who it was.

Quinn Briscoe.

The woman seemed to tower over Allie and the junkie, her blue eyes narrowing as she spoke. She was dressed in a military uniform, tannish green with an odd camouflage design that looked like it had been made by a computer. Even though the effect was thrown off slightly by the tray of onion rings and orange soda that she held, Allie was struck by the air of authority she projected. Quinn looked imposing as she stared down the junkie.

And hot, she thought.

"Nah, Sarge," the junkie muttered, his voice like gravel. "Me and the lady were just having a conversation." He took a step away from the table and towards Quinn. Not quite threatening, Allie thought, but obviously meant to intimidate.

Quinn was unfazed. She continued to glare at him, holding her ground.

“It’s Captain, actually,” she said in a low voice. “And the lady and I were just having lunch. You’re in *my* way right now and my onion rings are starting to get cold. I think you need to remove yourself from this situation.”

Quinn kept her eyes level with the junkie, her expression imperious as he stared back at her. The man finally gave a small shrug and then hobbled away, mumbling under his breath. Quinn watched him leave and then slid into the seat opposite Allie.

Allie stared at Quinn, not quite sure what to say.

Goddamn, that was fucking hot. Allie felt her cheeks flush at the thought.

“Um…thanks,” she said after a moment.

Quinn looked at her for a moment as if she might be considering something, nodded, and then picked up an onion ring. Allie looked down at her own plate of half-eaten fries then back at Quinn. She shook her head.

“Why…how are you here?” Allie asked. “I mean, first of all thank you. I’m not sure what…yeah, thank you for stepping in.” God she was flustered.

Quinn continued to eat her onion rings and then took a sip of orange soda. She eyed Allie for a few more minutes and then finally said, "Fort Mac."

"I'm sorry, what?"

"Fort Mac…Fort McPherson. I had some appointments there today. I decided to stop in and get a bite to eat on the way home."

"Oh." Allie had almost forgotten about the Army base just south of the city.

"I was sitting over there," Quinn motioned to the far side of the room. "I heard you talking on the phone, with I guess your boyfriend, and wasn't going to say anything if you didn't notice me. But then your friend came and here we are."

"No, that was my mother on my phone, actually." *Wait, what? Boyfriend?* "There's no boyfriend," she added quickly.

"Mmhmm. So, you're eating French fries?" Quinn said, motioning to Allie's plate with the last of the onion rings. Allie looked at her plate and then back at Quinn, nodding. "No onion rings?"

Allie shook her head. "No. I don't really like The Varsity's onion rings. Too greasy."

Quinn stopped in mid-chew and stared at her as if she'd suddenly grown a third eye.

"I knew that there was something wrong with you," she said.

Allie wasn't quite sure what to say to that, if it was meant as a joke or if the woman was serious. Looking across the table, Allie saw a flash of humor in Quinn's eyes as she took another sip of the soda.

So, that was a joke, then.

Allie's phone flashed and vibrated on the table. Seeing that it was her mother again, Allie ignored the call. She saw Quinn look at the phone but say nothing.

"Quinn, about the other day at your house…" Allie began. She'd thought about the exchange several times over the past few weeks. Amanda had been horrified when she recounted the conversation to her later that day on the ride home. The farther removed she got from the argument, the more embarrassed Allie had become about some of the things she said.

Quinn threw a palm up in the air and shook her head.

"Don't."

"But I just want to say—"

"I said don't. No point in rehashing things. We were both upset. I've thought about it a lot and I'm sure that you didn't really mean to tell me to go fuck myself any more than I really meant to call you a bitch."

"Actually you called me a rude ass bitch."

"I know," Quinn stated and swirled the ice around to get the last of the orange soda from the red paper cup.

Allie opened her mouth to respond when her cell phone began to flash and vibrate. Allie sighed and continued to ignore the phone.

"I don't think whoever that is calling is going away," Quinn said, glancing at the phone again.

"My mother," Allie lamented.

Quinn made a sound. "Aha. Have fun, then. I don't really talk to my mother, so I don't have to worry about calls like that."

"Oh, really?" Allie looked at the other woman and gave a small frown.

Quinn shrugged.

"Yeah, one of those things. I came out to my parents in college and neither she nor my father took it very well. I'm sure she saw all her dreams of grandchildren go up in flames at the word 'lesbian'. I think we went through a four or five year span where we didn't even talk."

Allie's mother drove her crazy and they maybe weren't on the best of terms at all times, but she couldn't imagine not having any sort of relationship with her. *Or not getting fifteen calls a day.*

“I’m sorry to hear that. You and Rebekah seem to be really close, though.”

“We are.” Quinn nodded, absently swirling around the ice in her cup. She looked up and flashed an odd smile at Allie. Quinn ran the back of one finger down her neck, tracing the raised angry scar. “And that whole me almost dying on the side of a mountain in Afghanistan thing made my parents realize that maybe there are worse things than having a lesbian for a daughter. We’re on a little bit better terms these days.” Allie really didn’t know what to say to that and shifted in her seat uncomfortably. Quinn must have noted, because she added, “Although…I still suspect my mom thinks that I’m going through a phase and just haven’t met the right guy yet.”

“Oh my goodness, doesn’t that sound familiar,” Allie laughed. “So…is that what happened, then? A helicopter crash? Not a MRE?” There was no point in pretending the scar wasn’t there given what had already been spoken between them.

“IED,” Quinn said with a faint laugh.

“Oh, it was an IED?”

“No, it was a helicopter crash. But you keep saying MRE when what you mean to say is IED—Improvised Explosive Device.”

"Ah, okay. I'm sorry, I probably should know more about things like that, but I don't. Most of my time is spent working. I don't watch a lot of television and when I do it's usually something like *Dancing with the Stars.*"

Allie's phone began to flash and vibrate again.

"You really should answer the phone, it looks like she is just going to keep calling until you do."

"I don't have anything to say to her right now. My sister is getting married next week in Asheville, North Carolina. Well, near there anyway," Allie explained. "The wedding is on Saturday. I've already made plans to make the five hour drive Friday evening. My sister and her fiancé are having a rehearsal luncheon on Wednesday and my mother is pissed that I'm not going to be there. I just can't stay the whole week. There's a Women's Expo at the Cobb Galleria that starts Friday morning. I have to be there for that, so there's no way I'm driving up there Tuesday night or early Wednesday morning, driving back Thursday, and then back up again on Friday. So, I'm just going to stop taking her calls until she gets the hint and leaves me alone about it."

Quinn nodded and then heaved a sigh.

"Well, it certainly has been an interesting lunch, but I really need to get back on the road if I'm going to miss rush hour traffic on the interstate."

Allie grinned. “It certainly has been interesting.” Quinn began to rise from the booth, but Allie motioned for her to stop. “Quinn, one thing?”

The other woman looked at her and raised an eyebrow.

“I’m not going to lie and say I’m sorry for everything that I said the other day, because I’m not. You did really piss me off. But, maybe some of that could have been said in a different way. Regardless, Rebekah is your sister and one of my designers, so I’d like for us to at least be cordial.”

Quinn twisted her lips and regarded Allie for a moment. Finally, she gave a small nod.

“I agree. I don’t see any problem with that.” She stood then and limped over to the trash bin to drop off her tray. She had begun to move towards the door when she stopped abruptly and turned to Allie.

It was Allie’s turn to raise an eyebrow.

“Do you want to go?”

“What? Where?”

“To the rehearsal luncheon. Do you want to go?”

Allie shrugged. “I’d like to, but it’s just not possible.”

“If you want to go, I can take you.” Allie realized she must have had a confused look on her face, because Quinn smirked and then explained, “I can fly you. It’d be like two hours there, two hours back. We can head up Wednesday morning and leave back out after lunch. I don't see well after dark anymore, so as long we are back in the air by three or four o'clock, it'll be no problem."

Allie frowned as she tried to wrap her mind around what Quinn was saying.

"Fly?" she asked hesitantly.

"Fly. In an airplane. I have a plane," Quinn said as if she was speaking to a child.

"Oh." It occurred to Allie that Quinn had just shared with her that she had crashed at least once before, so Allie wasn't sure how to say, "No, I'd rather not go down in a ball of flames just so I can eat chicken salad sandwiches with Aunt Marge," without insulting Quinn any further.

Quinn apparently read her mind because she said, "It's really very safe."

"Is it?" Allie asked, not really sure if she believed that or not.

"Yes, it is. Rebekah and I just flew up to Cherokee a month or so back. I can more or less use that flight plan. So long as we don't encounter any surface to air missiles over the Smoky Mountains, you have nothing to worry about."

"Well, I think we should be safe on that front," Allie said, smiling.

“Think about it,” Quinn said. “If you decide you want to do it, just call Rebekah and she can give you my number.”

Thinking that she may call Rebekah regardless to get Quinn’s number, Allie nodded.

“Okay. Thanks,” she said. “For everything.”

Quinn nodded. Looking like she wasn’t quite sure what else to say, she threw a hand up and then turned and limped out of the dining room. Allie watched wordlessly as she rounded the corner and disappeared from sight.

Well, Allie thought, w*hat do you know about that?*

Chapter Nine

"Okay, I think that's about as good as it's going to get."

Quinn nodded at Morales' words. She closed the lid on the first aid kit that she had been holding for the lanky Texan and tossed it to the ground beside her. He'd spent the better part of the last half hour applying gauze and hemostatic bandages to the gash on her neck in an attempt to stop the bleeding. The bandages, designed to clot blood on contact, itched and burned along the length of her neck. Hopefully a sign, Quinn told herself, that they were doing their job.

The kit that Morales had grabbed from the helicopter had given them more to work with than just the IFAK the young soldier kept attached to his flak jacket, but it was still woefully inadequate. The best they'd been able to do for her left leg was to tie off the bleeding below her knee with a tourniquet and wrap the rest in gauze and strips of Morales' t-shirt to try and keep the flies out. Quinn had passed out twice during the course of that little endeavor, but at least she was alive.

"How's your eye?" he asked quietly, moving to check again that the brush he had placed around the outcropping of rocks where they were positioned had not moved. The fifth time he left to check it she almost said something to him, but then realized that this wasn't a game of hide and seek that either of them could afford to lose. Better to be OCD than dead, she thought.

"Little better," she replied, rubbing one hand around her right eye. "I can at least see shapes out of it now, anyway."

"Good." He tapped the pistol sitting in her lap. "You gonna be able to see good enough to use that if comes to it?"

Quinn gave a short nod. "Oh, yeah." Exhausted and hurting, she closed her eyes and leaned her head back against the large boulder she was sitting in front of. "Still, you might want to stand behind me when the shooting starts, just to be on the safe side."

"The QRF guys will be coming out of J-Bad, so I hope to God they get off their ass and get here soon so we don't have to worry about that."

"I'm sure they will be," Quinn murmured, although she wasn't quite sure she believed her own words. Even if everything worked the way it was supposed to, they were at least an hour out from the base at Jalalabad. Assuming that the signal from the transponder had gone out and not taking into consideration what would be waiting for the reaction team at the crash site when they arrived.

Quinn shifted slightly and then drew in a sharp intake of breath as she unintentionally moved her leg.

“Bad?” Morales asked.

“Hurts like a motherfucker,” she answered in a strained voice.

Quinn really didn’t think a word existed that could adequately describe the pain that emanated from the lower area of her left leg. Excruciating? Agonizing? Once as a child she’d stepped in a bed of fire ants. That still didn’t come close to touching it. She’d caught a glimpse of the damage as Morales cut off what was left of her pant leg with the scissors from the helicopter’s first aid kit. Not much, but enough to make her stomach drop and bring up the bile to gag her again. There was a nasty gouge just below her knee that had been slowly pumping out blood. The area where her calf should be was just a shredded mess of skin and tissue that oddly reminded Quinn of the streamers that she’d had on the handlebars of that pink Schwinn back in elementary school. The skin around her ankle was flayed open and folded back, exposing the bone underneath.

“Well, look at it this way,” he began. “What is it that Keanu Reeves says in that movie? ‘Pain heals. Chicks dig scars. Glory lasts forever.’”

Quinn opened one eye to look at him and couldn’t help but laugh.

“Chicks dig scars, hmm? I’ll be sure to tell my girlfriend that.”

Morales raise an eye and scratched the side of his face with two blackened, bloodied fingers.

“Girlfriend, huh? I thought so. Fluffy—Specialist Pierce—said he was going to ask you to go out for a coffee with him when we got to Bagram. I told him he was wasting his time. Fucker owes me a beer.” Morales flashed a wry smile and Quinn saw a distant look of pain pass over his eyes.

“Well, I suppose I’ll have to pay up on his behalf, then,” she said quietly. He nodded, but didn’t say anything further. After a second he rose to check on their cover again.

“That’s not going to be a problem, is it Sergeant? Not that it really matters at this point.”

Morales looked at her and grinned, shaking his head.

“Naw, my Aunt Rosa is gay. I’m cool with it. She and her friends are always sending me packages of Little Debbies.”

“Mmm…wouldn’t an oatmeal cream pie be good right about now,” Quinn breathed, settling back against the cold rock.

"Naw, give me a nutty—" Morales stopped short and suddenly stiffened, tightening his grip on the rifle slung over his shoulder. "Did you hear that?"

Quinn tensed and cocked her head to listen. She could hear the noise, but only faintly. She picked up the pistol from her lap as she strained to better make out the sound.

It was a man's voice. He was looking for a lost shaker of salt.

Quinn sat up in the bed, knocking the calico cat off the side of her pillow as she moved. She caught her breath, muttered "Sonofabitch", and then reached to the side table to pick up her cell phone.

"Hello?" she said groggily into the phone.

"What the hell have you done?"

Quinn pulled the phone away from her ear, looked at the screen, and then held it back up to her head.

"Rebekah, do you know what time it is?"

Her sister continued on. "Yes, I know what time it is. Don't try to change the subject. What have you done?"

One of these days…

"Do I even want to guess what you're talking about?" she asked, falling back onto the soft bed.

"I got a text message from Allie Jenkins asking if I could forward her your number." Quinn had a fleeting image of golden brown hair and pink lips and was surprised to find herself smiling. “Oh.”

“Oh? Don’t *oh* me, Quinn. What have you done that she would be asking for your number?”

“I haven’t done anything, Rebekah, give it a rest.”

“Then why does she want *your* number all of a sudden?”

“Why is it so strange that someone would be asking for my number?”

“Quinn, I swear to God—”

“We had lunch together the other day,” Quinn interrupted.

“What?”

“Did I stutter?”

“No, but…what do you mean you had lunch together? Where?”

“At The Varsity. I was coming back up from Fort Mac and stopped in for lunch. She was there. We talked.”

“Quinn, what did you say to her? You didn’t say anything insulting to her, did you? I know what you call her.”

“What, a rude bitch?” Quinn smirked.

“You did not fucking call her a rude bitch. Tell me you didn’t.”

“Goddamn, Rebekah, of course not.” She heard her sister give an exasperated sigh on the other end of the phone.

"Then why is she asking for your number?"

Quinn decided that she wasn't going to get back to sleep, so sat up and began to make her way to the kitchen in search of coffee.

"Her sister is getting married," she explained as she padded through the living room. "She's got some kinda expo or something on Friday, so was going to have to miss the rehearsal lunch because she didn't have time to drive up to North Carolina and back. I offered to take her up in the one seventy-two."

There was a silence on the other end of the phone.

"You did what?" Rebekah asked.

"I offered to fly her up there and back. I got the impression that she thought it was a bad idea, so I told her to think about it and call you for my number if she changed her mind."

"I'm confused."

Quinn sighed as she flipped the switch on the coffee pot. She leaned one hip against the counter and rubbed her eyes. "What is confusing about that?"

"Nothing…it's just…why—"

"Why would I offer to do that?"

"Yes."

"Aren't you always telling me to be nice to people?"

“Well, yes, but you never actually do it.”

“Whatever.” Quinn walked to the refrigerator and opened the door, pulling out a small container of creamer.

“I didn’t mean it like that,” Rebekah said. “I’m just surprised that you’re finally doing it, is all. And…with Allie Jenkins of all people.”

“I’m your sister and you’re one of her designers. I figured we could at least be cordial,” Quinn said, mimicking Allie’s words from the restaurant. There was another silence on the other end of the phone. “Are you still there?” Quinn said after a few moments passed.

“Yes,” Rebekah said quietly. “I think I’m going to cry.”

“Rebekah, it’s not that big of a deal.”

Her sister said nothing and Quinn was pretty sure she heard a sniffle.

Oh, goddamn.

“Did you give her the number?” she asked.

“What?”

“My number. You said she asked for the number. Did you give it to her?”

“Oh,” Rebekah answered. “I did.”

“All right, well great. I’m hanging up now,” she said and then hit the END button on the phone. Quinn dropped it on the countertop and then reached up to grab a cup out of the cabinet.

Huh, she thought as poured the hot, black coffee from the carafe into a cup. *How about that?*

Chapter Ten

Allie stood quietly looking over the small, blue and white striped plane parked on the—Runway? Tarmac? What did you call it?—at the Pickens County, Georgia, airport. It wasn't an airport in any sense that Allie was used to. There was no baggage check, no ticket counter, just a relatively small, nondescript building surrounded by a few white metal hangars.

She wondered, not for the first time that day, what she was getting herself into. She had already decided she was going to turn down Quinn's offer, when she made the mistake of mentioning the entire incident to Amanda. Before she knew it, Amanda had snatched up Allie's cell phone, started texting like a crazy person, and then told Allie that she wasn't going to let her 'fuck this up a third time'.

Quinn, looking very business casual in a pair of tan slacks and a pale green collared shirt, was walking around the plane with a clipboard. She opened the plane's hood and glanced up at Allie.

Grinning, she said, "I'm almost done with the pre-flight inspect and then we'll be good to go. Seriously, don't look so worried. It's all perfectly safe."

Allie flushed, a little embarrassed that her discomfort was so obvious. She shifted the large yellow tote slung over one shoulder and then took a step towards the front of the plane. She peered up over the side and into the engine compartment.

"Oh, I know. You've said. I'm sure I'll be fine." Allie was surprised how simple the engine looked. And small. "What are you looking at?" she asked, trying not to think about the fact that that small little piece of machinery would be the only thing keeping them from plummeting to the ground.

"It's been a month or so since I've taken her up, so I'm just making sure no birds have built nests in the engine cowling," Quinn said matter-of-factly as she closed the hood.

Fuck. This. Shit.

Allie turned and was about to run back to her car when she heard Quinn say, "Okay, let's get moving."

I can do this, I can do this, I can do this.

"Great," she said, swallowing hard and following in behind Quinn. The other woman opened the door on the right side of the plane and motioned for Allie to get in. Placing one foot on a small step just over the landing gear for balance, she eased into the cockpit, sitting gingerly onto a gray leather seat. She looked at the dash covered in switches and dials and took a deep breath to steel her resolve.

Allie glanced over as Quinn sat in the seat opposite hers and began to flip switches and push buttons.

"Ready?" the other woman asked. Allie nodded and then jumped as Quinn suddenly popped her head out the side window and yelled, "Clear prop!"

Quinn turned a key and then pushed a few more buttons. She revved the engine and then looked over the dials on the instrument panel. Reaching down between the seats, she picked up and handed Allie a headset.

"Here," she said. "Put this on. It can get a little loud in the cockpit." Allie nodded and placed the headset on, feeling a little like she was about to play one of Nicky's video games. Her stomach lurched as she felt the plane begin to move. She closed her eyes and tried to ignore the bumps as the small plane turned and began to pick up speed. Her nose twitched at the smell of fuel, oil, and leather that drifted through the cockpit.

Allie heard Quinn's voice speaking through the headset. "Atlanta Approach, Cessna seven four six tango poppa requesting flight following." There was the sound of static and then a man's voice began answering, spouting out numbers.

She finally opened her eyes to see Quinn turning a dial on the instrument panel. Allie turned her head and glanced out the small window on the door to her right. Her breath caught as she took in the sight below. They were flying over tree covered hills. The roads and houses looked tiny, like something out of a model train set. Looking up, she realized she could see for miles in either direction. The sky was incredibly blue and the clouds little puffs of smoke.

"This is amazing!"

She heard Quinn laugh.

"That's what everybody says their first time up," she said. "And you don't have to yell, I can hear you just fine through the headset."

"Oh, I'm sorry," Allie said, embarrassed.

"No, it's okay."

"So, what were those numbers that man said back there when we took off? I couldn't make it all out clearly."

"That was our squawk code. I enter it into the transponder and that allows Atlanta air traffic control to monitor us on radar. They will advise of any other planes that may be flying close by, any bad weather ahead…any surface to air missile batteries in the area." Allie looked over at Quinn at that last. She was grinning. Her blue eyes danced teasingly as she continued, "I told you it would be fine."

Allie did have to admit that it was nothing like she'd thought it would be. The ride was surprising smooth, nothing like the big airliners she had flown on in the past.

"You were right, I have to admit. I don't think I've ever known anyone who owned their own airplane."

"I've had it for years. It's not the biggest or the best, but it gets me from Point A to Point B. I picked it up just after my first deployment."

"Your first deployment? How many times were you deployed?"

Quinn shrugged. "All depends on how you look at it, I guess. I've been assigned to a few different places around the states, but most of my time has been at Fort Rucker." At Allie's inquiring look, she added, "That's in Alabama. I did one tour in Iraq and two in Afghanistan. I also spent a few months in Georgia—the country not the state—on training missions."

"Wow," Allie said, not sure what to say.

Quinn nodded and adjusted something on the control panel.

"I went to France one time when I was in high school," Allie suddenly found herself blurting out. *Oh my God, did I really just say that?*

Quinn eyed her for a moment then let out a loud laugh.

"So, you said your aunt and uncle are going to meet us at the airport in Asheville?"

"Yes. The lodge where the wedding and all the festivities are going to be is about thirty minutes north of there, so hopefully they won't talk our ears off on the car ride up."

"Our ears? I figured I'd just stay around the airport."

Allie frowned at Quinn.

"Oh. Quinn, you don't have to do that. You are more than welcome to come to the lunch."

Quinn shrugged. "No, really. It wasn't my intention to invite myself to your family thing when I offered to fly you up here."

For a moment Allie thought about what Amanda would say if she allowed Quinn to stay at some dirty airport rather than accompany her to the romantic lodge nestled in the mountains of North Carolina, even if it was just for the rehearsal lunch.

"Seriously, there is no point in you hanging around the airport. I've been hearing the great debate of chicken salad over tuna salad for weeks now. Please come and eat with us. It's the least I can do after you came to the rescue the other day and now…taking the time to fly me all the way up here."

Quinn trained her eyes on the blue sky in front of them for a few moments before she answered.

"I don't think that would actually constitute a rescue, but okay. If you don't think anyone from your family would mind."

"Of course not. And I wouldn't care if they did."

"Well, all right then." Quinn suddenly motioned to the cabin behind them. "Oh, I got you a present."

Allie's narrowed her eyes and tried to ignore the warm feeling that spread across her chest at Quinn's words.

"A present? What do you mean?"

"Right there behind you on the cabin floor. Go ahead."

Allie frowned and turned around in the seat. She caught a glimpse of a brown object on the floor in front of the rear seat bench. She reached down and picked it up and then straightened back into her seat. She held the object—a heavy, brown rectangular package of some sort—at arm's length to read the words stamped on the outside.

"Chicken fajita tortilla," she read. "What is this?"

Quinn grinned. "It's a MRE. Meal ready to eat. As many times as you've mentioned them to me, I figured I'd get you one."

"Oh my God, I'm so embarrassed," Allie said, feeling her cheeks flush. "I can't believe I asked if you'd gotten blown up by a MRE. Chicken fajita tortilla."

She could hear Quinn chuckling over the headset.

"Don't be embarrassed. I thought it was funny. That's one of my favorite flavors, by the way, comes with the Irish cream coffee mix."

"I may never live this down," she said, smiling back at Quinn.

"Well, you're going to have to. We're just about to make our approach."

Allie popped her head and looked out the window.

"What? Already?"

"I told you it would be quick trip," Quinn replied as she began to turn knobs on the instrument panel. "Asheville tower, Cessna seven four six tango poppa is ten miles to the south, inbound for full stop."

Allie leaned towards the window and gazed down at the scenery as Quinn continued to talk into the headset. It was a beautiful area with rolling hills and valleys. Little streams dotted the landscape, with the occasional farm house peeking out from behind the trees. She'd driven through the area several times in the past, but never had this particular vantage point before.

"Oh my goodness, it's beautiful isn't it?" she said.

Allie looked back over to find Quinn watching her.

"It certainly is."

Chapter Eleven

Half-listening to Allie's Aunt Marge drone on over whether the waitress with the blonde hair and big boobs had given her the evil eye, Quinn realized that, though she'd been to her fair share of funerals, she'd been to only a handful of weddings. "That girl had a definite attitude. I know attitude when I see it. All I asked her to do was turn down the air conditioning in here before we all froze to death. Did you see that look she gave me?"

"Yes, dear." For his part, Allie's Uncle Barney seemed resigned to his fate and gave the occasional affirmative response as he absently piled tuna salad on top of crackers.

As she thought on it some more, she finally settled on the number three. Her older sister Erin's elaborate wedding, the Las Vegas wedding chapel ceremony of her college roommate, and the on-post wedding of one of the Lieutenants in her squadron just before they shipped out to Afghanistan the first time. While the last two had required very little effort on her part, Erin's wedding had a week-long, tortuous exercise filled with lace and pink taffeta.

"What do you think Quinn?"

It took a moment for Quinn to realize that Aunt Marge was asking her opinion on something, although for the life of her she had no idea what. Quinn raised up in the seat and looked over at the elderly woman with big hair and a sparkling sequined blue blouse.

"I'm sorry, what?" she asked.

"Allie," the woman said, chewing on dip-covered potato chip.

Quinn glanced to Uncle Barney for help. He shrugged and shook his head, apparently as lost as she was.

"What about Allie?"

"Does she have any prospects?"

"Prospects for what?" Quinn looked at Uncle Barney again. In response he handed her a tuna salad cracker.

"You know, prospects. I figured that you're a friend of hers, that you would know."

"Uh, well…I don't know that we're that good friends," she said nibbling on the cracker. *Not bad,* she thought and reached for another from Uncle Barney's outstretched hand.

"Surely you must have some idea of whether or not she has some prospect of a man out there. As pretty as she is, there has got to be somebody."

Quinn swallowed hard on the bite of tuna salad she was eating and reached for the glass of Diet Coke on the table in front of her, coughing slightly.

“I really don’t know,” she said. Quinn glanced across the ballroom until her eyes fell on Allie, lined up by the stage next to three other women and her sister Taylor. They were getting directions from the perky wedding coordinator dressed in a white shirt and pink pants that were a size too small on what they were to do during the ceremony on Saturday.

“Well, she’s not getting any younger,” Aunt Marge continued, dipping another chip into the French onion dip.

“I don’t think she’s into men, Marge,” Uncle Barney said, speaking for the first time. Quinn snapped her head back towards the gruff voice and then accepted another tuna cracker from the man with overly black hair and a Member’s Only jacket.

Aunt Marge made a tutting sound.

“Don’t be silly, Barney. What does that even mean? She’s not into men?”

“I mean I don’t think she’s into men. You know, one of those.”

“One of those what?” Aunt Marge said.

Yeah, Quinn thought, *one of those what?* She still wasn’t quite sure where this conversation was going to lead, so decided her best course was to say as little as possible.

“You know, Lebanese,” he answered.

Quinn coughed, nearly choking on the tuna cracker she was eating. Both Marge and Barney looked at her with raised eyebrows as she reached again for the Diet Coke.

Oh, hell.

"Really, Barney, what's gotten into you? She's not Lebanese, she was born in Tennessee. Or was that Taylor? One of those girls was born in Tennessee."

"What does that have to do with anything?" he mumbled. He carefully spooned out the last of the tuna salad onto a cracker and handed it to Quinn.

"Well, you said she was Lebanese."

"What else would you call it?"

"What else would you call what?" Aunt Marge questioned, swirling around the last sip of wine in her glass.

"Not being into men. Lebanese."

"Barney that doesn't make any sense. What do you mean Lebanese? Like Casey Kasem?"

"Lesbian," Quinn barked out across the table.

Barney and Marge turned to her, both saying, "What?" at the same time as if they hadn't heard her. Quinn sighed, ignoring the stares from the table next to them, who obviously *had* heard. The occupants of that table, Taylor's cousins from West Virginia, were already on her list, having openly pointed to Quinn's neck and whispered amongst one another when she and Allie had arrived at the lodge with Barney and Marge earlier. They could go to hell for all she was concerned.

"Lesbian," Quinn repeated in a low voice. "That's what you call a woman who is not into men."

Aunt Marge frowned at her and then slugged down the last of her wine.

"Allie is a lesbian?"

"I didn't say Allie is a lesbian. Barney kept calling it 'Lebanese'. The word is lesbian, not Lebanese."

"That's what I said," Uncle Barney said, spooning chicken salad onto his plate. He took a big scoop and offered it to Quinn, who shook her head. "Lesbian."

"Well, that doesn't make any sense at all. How could Allie be a lesbian? Look how pretty she is," Aunt Marge declared.

Quinn sighed, suddenly feeling very hot. *I should have kept my mouth shut.*

"Again, I didn't say Allie is a lesbian. She might be, she might not be. I have no idea. I was just telling you what the right word was."

"Maybe Quinn lesbians with Allie," Uncle Barney offered up as he swallowed a spoonful of chicken salad. He motioned to Quinn with the spoon. "She's got the short hair."

"Quinn? Do you lesbian with Allie?" Aunt Marge asked, looking up and down at Quinn.

"Lesbian is not a verb. You cannot 'lesbian' someone. That doesn't even make sense," Quinn said, restraining the urge to start hitting her head against the table.

"Well, it would be okay if you did lesbian with her. You seem like a nice young woman. Allie needs a good prospect. Maybe you two can adopt a baby like those girls on television, you know."

"No, I don't know, Aunt Marge." Quinn began to feel nauseous. She looked back across the room at Allie. Allie met her eyes and gave a small wave.

"Oh, you know. What's the name of that show Barney? It comes on right before the news."

"I don't know what you're talking about. You know I don't watch television."

"You most certainly do watch television. What do you call staying up past midnight to watch the Atlanta Braves?"

"That's not television, that's baseball."

Quinn rested her elbows on the table and then put her head on her hands. She could feel a sheen of perspiration spread across her forehead. Her stomach started to rumble ominously.

“Do you know where the restroom is?” she croaked to Aunt Marge and Uncle Barney.

“I think it’s over there by the door to the kitchen,” Aunt Marge said. “Are you okay, honey? You don’t look so good.”

“No, I don’t feel so good all of a sudden.” Quinn took a deep breath and stood slowly from the table, afraid that if she moved too fast she would throw up. Or worse.

“Oh, honey, you are green.” Quinn felt Marge come up beside her and grab onto her arm. “Barney go get Allie. Tell her Quinn’s not feeling well. I’m going to take her to the restroom,” the older woman said as she led Quinn to the other side of the ballroom.

Quinn groaned as she felt her stomach roll and the room begin to slowly sway.

Aunt Marge tightened her grip on Quinn’s arm and made a tutting sound.

“Don’t worry, honey, we’re almost there,” she said encouragingly.

“Is everything okay?”

Quinn started as Allie’s father suddenly materialized between them and the door to the restroom. He frowned with concern and reached a hand out to help steady her. She was about to open her mouth to say that she would be okay if she could just get to the restroom when Aunt Marge interrupted.

"No, Alan, she's gotten sick all of a sudden. I bet it was all that tuna salad she was eating. I thought it smelled funny."

Now is a hell of a time to say something about that.

"Can I help you get her to the restroom?"

"No, I've got her. Barney went to go get Allie," Aunt Marge told him.

"Allie?" he asked, turning back towards the stage as he ran a hand across his short, salt and pepper hair.

"Yes," Aunt Marge said and then added in a whisper, "She and Allie lesbian together."

Quinn vomited all over the ballroom floor.

Chapter Twelve

"Okay, just one more step."

Allie held the hotel door as her father half-carried, half-drug a semi-conscious Quinn into the room. The heavy-set man grunted as they crossed the threshold and then leaned her against the wall. He looked at Allie as he took a breath.

"I guess I should be grateful she's not as big as your last girlfriend."

"For God sakes, Dad, she's not my girlfriend."

"That's not what your Aunt Marge says."

"Aunt Marge is insane."

He shook his head and picked up Quinn again. "Which way?"

"Over here," Allie said as she walked through the small living room area and opened the door that led to the bedroom. Alan Jenkins heaved Quinn up and onto the king-sized bed that sat in the corner of the room. She landed on her stomach with a soft moan.

"Is it time to go to school?" she murmured, lifting her head off the mattress.

Allie sighed. They had spent the better part of the last five hours at the emergency room. Quinn apparently had the worst case of food poisoning in the history of North Carolina, or at least to hear Aunt Marge talk she did.

"No, it's not. Just try to get some sleep," she instructed. Quinn groaned softly and then let her head fall back down.

"The doctor said the shot should knock her out for a while," Allie's father said, turning and walking out of the bedroom. He reached into his shirt pocket and pulled out a small pill bottle. He placed it on the counter of the kitchenette that sat adjacent to the living room. "Here's those pills he gave us in case she starts throwing up again."

"I don't think they're pills, Dad," Allie said tersely.

"Lord. Have fun with that," he said. He heaved a sigh and ran a hand through his hair. "Do you need anything else?"

Allie shook her head. "No. Mom said on the phone she and Taylor brought some clothes up to the room while we were at the hospital. I think she said she was going to put some drinks in the fridge too. I've already called Quinn's sister and let her know what's going on. I think we should be fine from here."

"Well, call if you need anything. We're in room three-twelve," he said and then leaned forward, kissing Allie gently on the forehead. "Goodnight."

"Night Dad," Allie echoed, closing the door behind him.

What a hell of a day.

Allie turned back towards the bedroom and sighed, rubbing the back of her neck with one hand. Allie sat down on the bed beside Quinn and took a breath while she surveyed the situation. The unconscious woman hadn't moved from the position she left her in and was still face down on the bed. Allie glanced around the room, looking for and finding the stack of clothes left by her mother sitting on the chair by the bed. She decided there wasn't a lot else to do other than get Quinn changed out of the vomit-stained clothes. After that, she would get setup on the couch in the living room and try to get some sleep herself.

No time like the present.

"Okay, Quinn. We gotta get you out of these clothes. You're going to have to help me a little bit here," she said, standing and walking to the edge of the bed. She pulled off one of Quinn's shoes and tossed it on the floor. Quinn made a noise as Allie tugged off the other shoe and let it drop.

"Uhhmmm," Quinn moaned.

"Quinn…" Allie said, patting her on the back and then walking over to the chair. "C'mon. Let's go, it won't take but a minute and then we'll be done."

"I don't want to go. It hurts too much…just go without me…"

"No, you're going to have to help a little bit," Allie answered. She went through the clothes, picked up a bright pink t-shirt, and carried it back to the bed. She hooked the bottom of Quinn's shirt and then pulled it up towards her head. "Quinn, raise your arms."

"Damn it Morales, stop it."

"It's not Morales, Quinn, it's Allie. Help me out. We can leave your bra on, but this shirt has got to go."

"Allie?"

"Yes, Allie," she answered exasperated.

"Mmmm, Allie," Quinn mumbled. "Pretty lips."

Allie stilled.

"What?"

"You have pretty pink lips," Quinn breathed and rolled over on the bed. She looked at Allie, her eyes half-open and glassy. "I've been wanting to kiss them," she whispered and then reached up and pulled Allie down to her. Quinn crushed her mouth against Allie's at the same time she wrapped her hands behind Allie's head.

Quinn's fingers ran through Allie's hair as she deepened the kiss. Allie found her mouth opening of its own accord to Quinn's tongue. She flicked it against Allie's, teasing and tasting as Allie whimpered at the hot ache that began to build just below her stomach. With a groan, Allie tore away from the kiss and pushed Quinn back onto the bed.

I deserve a goddamn medal for this.

"Quinn, we can't do this, sweetie."

In response, Quinn sighed and closed her eyes. Allie shook her head and finished pulling Quinn's shirt off, willing herself to ignore both the woman's white lacy bra and the supple breasts that seemed to be begging to be touched. She grabbed the t-shirt and kneeled on the bed beside Quinn. For the first time she got an up close look at the scar on the other woman's neck and was surprised by its length. The puckered pink scar ran in a jagged line from the edge of her jaw almost to her collarbone. She was amazed that whatever had done the damage had not killed the woman outright. Allie flushed as she realized she was unconsciously tracing the scar with the tip of one finger. She drew her hand back quickly, flashing a quick look to make sure that Quinn was still asleep. She grimaced and eased the t-shirt over Quinn's head, pulling it down in one quick movement.

Halfway there.

She gripped Quinn under the arms and began to pull her towards the head of the bed.

"Little bit more, Quinn. Let's get you to where you won't roll over and fall off the bed tonight," Allie said loudly, trying to wake the sleeping woman enough to help her.

Quinn moaned and batted at Allie's hands.

"Leave me here. Just go," she muttered.

"C'mon Quinn, almost there," Allie grunted.

"Mmmnnn," Quinn moaned. "Stop, leave me. You're gonna get yourself killed. I'm already dead…just go."

Allie stopped and looked at Quinn. She found the woman staring back at her with vacant eyes. It occurred to her that in Quinn's drug-dulled mind she must think herself back in Afghanistan, and she did not want to go back there with her. She bit her bottom lip while she considered her next move. Allie decided that Quinn was far enough towards the middle of the bed that she shouldn't be able to roll over and fall off during the night. She would just slide off the semi-conscious woman's pants, cover her with the blanket, and call it a night.

"Okay sweetie, I'm going to leave you here, okay?"

"Mmmnn…" Quinn closed her eyes and lay back on the bed.

Allie undid the button of Quinn's pants and slid the zipper down. She grinned wryly, thinking that she could honestly tell Amanda that she'd managed to get Quinn out of her pants on the first date.

Date from hell, she thought. Although, that kiss was pretty nice. Well, more than just pretty nice, but she'd rather not take advantage of someone so clearly not in their right mind, no matter how hot they were.

Allie gripped the legs of the tan pants and pulled down, sliding them off in one fluid motion. She tossed the pants next to Quinn's shoes and reached to pull the blanket over her. Quinn moaned and shifted on the bed. Allie caught a glimpse of Quinn's left leg then and froze.

She'd thought that after the episode in the ballroom and, then later at the hospital, there was not a lot left that would be able to turn her stomach. Looking at the patchwork of tissue and muscle that made up Quinn's lower leg, she realized that she'd been wrong. Allie swallowed, pushing back the bile as she took it all in. There was no calf, that portion of her leg was simply gone. Its absence seemed to emphasize what was left, the flesh that appeared to be stretched and stitched haphazardly in some Frankenstein-like effort to cover bone. And then her ankle… It hurt her to think of the suffering Quinn must have gone through. Must still be going through.

Allie closed her eyes and took a breath. Compelling herself to not to look any further, she opened her eyes and then reached again for the blanket. She covered the sleeping woman and then just stood there, peering down at her face.

Quinn looked incredibly peaceful passed out on the king-sized bed. It was a stark contrast to the torment that Allie knew she had to have endured after the helicopter crash. She'd never imagined such a thing possible.

Wiping back tears, Allie turned and walked out of the bedroom, closing the door behind her.

Chapter Thirteen

Quinn felt like her face was fire. The heat was unbearable and, no matter which way she turned, she couldn't escape it. It burned her eyes and scorched her throat. She felt her lips crack and bleed with dehydration.

She slowly became aware that she was lying on something uncomfortably soft. She frowned and began to feel around her, tentatively at first and then spreading her arms wide, her fingers touching what felt like cool cotton sheets. Realizing she was in a bed—and not her own—she forced her eyes open and instantly threw a hand up to shield them. She blinked at the bright sunlight that was streaming through the burgundy curtains that covered a tall window on the other side of the room.

Quinn sat up in the bed, looking at the strange room around her. The walls were wood-paneled, a light pine color. There was a dresser of the same color wood and a tan wingback chair sitting in one corner. She noted a door on either end of the room. Through the one that was opened she could just make out the edge of a bathtub. As she drew back the blanket, she realized that she wore a bright pink t-shirt that read "UGA Gal" under a large bulldog's face. And nothing else.

What. The. Fuck.

She eased off the bed, taking a hesitant step onto the brown plush carpet. She raked her eyes across the room, looking for something that would jog her memory of where she was and how she got there. Noting only her shoes lined up neatly by the closed door, she stretched the pink t-shirt down as far down as the fabric would go and cautiously turned the door handle.

Quinn eased open the door and peeked out, not quite sure what to expect. It certainly wasn't a smiling Allie standing behind the bar of what looked to be a kitchenette, slathering peanut butter onto a bagel.

"Well, hello there, sleepyhead," Allie grinned at her and then turned to drop the knife she had been holding into a sink. "How are you feeling?"

"Umm…a little tired, to tell you the truth."

Quinn looked around and realized they were in a hotel room of some sort. It was a large room, with walls of the same light colored pine as in the bedroom. A marble-top bar separated the kitchenette from the living area. They seemed to be alone in the room. Quinn began to rub the back of her neck with one hand, but then realized in doing so the pink t-shirt was riding up along her hips. She quickly pulled it back down.

"Where are my pants?" she asked, her voice faltering.

From behind the bar Allie crossed her arms and then gave what Quinn's grandfather used to call a shit-eating grin.

"You have no idea what happened, do you?" she asked.

Quinn padded to the one of the black leather stools that sat along the edge of the bar and sat down.

"Not a damn clue." Quinn frowned and tried to recall what she had been doing just before she woke up in that bed wearing this god-awful t-shirt. She had a fleeting image of Allie's Uncle Barney handing her a cracker.

"You don't remember asking me to marry you?" Allie asked softly.

"What?"

"I'm sorry," Allie giggled, "I couldn't resist." She ignored the evil look that garnered from Quinn and continued. "You got food poisoning."

"Food poisoning?"

Allie nodded. "Bad tuna salad. Luckily—or maybe unluckily, I guess it depends on how you look at it—no one else but you ate any of it. Everyone else had the chicken salad. We had to take you to the hospital and they gave you a shot to stop the vomiting. It pretty much knocked you on your ass."

Quinn bit her lower lip and squinted as she tried to remember. It all came back to her in pieces. Uncle Barney handing her tuna salad on a cracker. Aunt Marge walking her across the ballroom. Allie's father…

"Oh my God, Aunt Marge told your dad that you and I lesbian together," Quinn blurted, the blood leaving her face.

Allie's faced puckered. "Lesbian together?" She laughed and shook her head. "Aunt Marge is insane."

"God, Allie. I'm so sorry. I didn't mean to out you to your family. I mean…I don't know if I did or if you are gay or not. I mean, I kinda thought your were…but you've never come out and said you were…and then Marge was talking about prospects and Barney started talking about Lebanese…and then there was something about the Atlanta Braves…"

Oh God, I'm babbling.

"I'm gay."

Quinn snapped her head up to look at Allie.

"What?"

The other woman smiled and nodded her head. "I'm a lesbian. It's okay, you didn't out me. My family knows, or most of them do anyway. I don't make a secret of it. It's not a big deal."

Quinn stared at her wordlessly. She wasn't sure if it was the fact that it *had been* such a big deal in her own family, or the way that Allie's eyes seemed to dance when she spoke.

A sudden thought struck her.

"Allie, where are my pants?" Quinn glanced down at the god-awful pink t-shirt. "And my shirt, for that matter."

"I'm thinking your shirt may have been incinerated. There's only so much that Tide will get out. Your pants are on the chair in the bedroom with some donated clothes from my sister and my mother. The hotel laundry brought them back up yesterday."

Quinn froze.

"Yesterday? What do you mean yesterday? What is today?"

"Friday," Allie said and then took a bite of the bagel. "You want some coffee?" she asked, motioning to the counter behind her. "There's about half a pot left."

"Friday?" Quinn said incredulously. "But…no, it was Wednesday and…how is this Friday?"

Allie swallowed. "I told you, that shot knocked you on your ass. You've been out of it for the past day and a half, give or take."

"But, no…" Quinn was having a hard time wrapping her head around it. "My cat!" *Lord, did I really just say that?*

“I called your sister and she’s taking care of him.”

“The expo? You had the expo on Friday.”

“I called and made other arrangements.”

“But…”

“Hey,” Allie said gently, reaching a hand out to cover Quinn’s. “Don’t worry, it’s all covered.”

Quinn looked at the soft hand touching her own and then raised her eyes to Allie’s. She already knew the answer, but had to know for certain.

“Allie, who undressed me?” she asked quietly.

Allie took another bite of the bagel before answering. She stepped back and chewed carefully as she stared at Quinn.

“I did.”

Quinn wasn’t sure why, but she began to feel hot. She shifted uncomfortably on the leather barstool.

“Thank you,” she said stiffly, looking down to stare at the speckled marble of the bar. She knew it shouldn’t bother her that Allie had seen her…seen all of her, the hideous sight that was her left leg. Her cheeks stung as she had a sudden flash of memory, that last argument with Laurie and the words that the woman who had stood by her bedside all those weeks at the hospital professing her love had spit out just before walking out the door. *Disgusting. Revolting. Makes me want to throw up.*

Quinn started as she felt soft fingers wrap around her wrist.

"Hey," Allie said lightly. "Are you okay?"

Quinn nodded and straightened up on the stool.

"I'm fine, thank you. I really appreciate you taking care of all this. I know how incredibly embarrassing it must have all been for you."

Allie held her gaze, but did not release her grip on Quinn's wrist.

"Quinn, can I ask two questions?"

She raised an eyebrow and shrugged. "Sure, I suppose so."

"Did Morales make it off the mountain?"

If Allie hadn't been holding onto her wrist, Quinn might've fallen off the bar stool.

"What?" she didn't so much ask as breathe.

"Sergeant Morales. Did he make it off the mountain, or did something happen to him?"

For a long moment, neither of them spoke.

"How?" Quinn questioned, shaking her head.

"You talk in your sleep. A lot. You carried on several conversations with Sergeant Morales over the past two days and he seemed to be a very nice person. You mentioned some others, but I got the impression that none of them made it out, so I was curious what happened to him."

Quinn opened her mouth, but seemed to have a hard time putting words together. She blinked as she felt tears well up in eyes.

"No, he made it. The QRF finally came and got us out of there...quick-reaction force. Like John Wayne and the Calvary in those old movies," she said at Allie's inquiring look. "He's okay. Actually had couple broken ribs as it turned out from what I understand, but he never let on that he was injured. Of course, I was pretty out of it, so…"

"Well good," Allie said, smiling.

Quinn nodded.

Allie continued to grasp Quinn's wrist and slowly began to rub circles on her arm with the tip of one finger. Quinn watched, feeling tiny shivers run up her arm with each delicate touch.

"He was right, you know," Allie said in a low voice.

"About what?" Quinn was hypnotized by the movement of the other woman's finger.

"Some chicks do dig scars."

Quinn froze. “What?” She wasn’t quite sure if she actually said the word, or just thought it, as Allie made no indication that she had heard her.

“I don’t know how else to say it,” Allie said, finally breaking the silence, her face expressionless. “I’ll be honest with you, when I…when I got an up close and personal look at your leg and this…” Her voice trailed off as she released Quinn’s wrist. Quinn stiffened as Allie’s eyes met hers and she felt a touch begin to run down her neck, following the uneven path of the scar. “…I really didn’t know what to think.”

“Really,” Quinn murmured.

“Really,” Allie answered with a smile. “Except to know that the more I’m with you, the less I see…this…” The touch became a caress and slowly moved to the nape of Quinn’s neck. “…and the more I just see…you. And, I’d like to see more of you. If you’ll let me.”

“Allie, I…” she began, her voice faltering as Allie deepened her caress and she felt her eyes close of their own accord. Quinn felt a warmth like liquid fire spread from Allie’s touch, threatening to consume her.

Quinn shifted on the barstool and she felt cool air run across her bare legs. She pulled back from Allie and shook her head as if she’d been in a trance.

I can't do this.

"I, uh, think I need to go get dressed," she said in a strained voice.

Allie lowered her eyes and nodded. "I understand," she said flatly and leaned back off the bar. Picking up the half-forgotten bagel, she took a small bite.

Quinn stood from the barstool and began to move back towards the bedroom. She ignored the familiar throbbing in her left ankle as she walked. For once, the smoldering pain that plagued her was overshadowed by a deeper, hotter ache that seemed to burn from the nape of her neck all the way to her core. As she reached the doorway, she stopped. What the fuck was she doing?

"What was the other question?" she asked, staring straight ahead. She could see her reflection through the mirror in the bathroom.

"What?"

"You said you wanted to ask two questions. What was the other question?"

"I don't suppose it's important now."

"I'd like to hear it."

There was the briefest moment of silence, and then Allie stepped up behind Quinn. They stared at one another through the reflection in the mirror.

“I was going to ask if you liked peanut butter.”

“Well, I can honestly say I never saw that one coming. Peanut butter?”

“Mmmhmm,” Allie said, taking a step closer to Quinn, her eyes darkening. “I just wanted to make sure that you weren’t maybe allergic to peanuts or anything.”

“Um, no, I’m not allergic to peanuts,” Quinn frowned. She felt her breath hitch as Allie’s hand slowly began to run up her back.

“Well, after the tuna salad incident, I didn’t want to do anything else that might send you back to the hospital.”

Quinn turned to face Allie and suddenly found herself being pushed against the living room wall, Allie’s lips pressing hard against hers. She kissed her open-mouthed, Allie’s lips seeming to devour her own. Quinn caught the faint taste of peanut butter as her tongue sparred with Allie’s. She felt her body mold against the other woman’s, heat exploding everywhere Allie’s hands moved. Allie deepened the kiss, turning her hot lips to the soft skin along Quinn’s ear and neck. Quinn gasped, trying to take in a breath as Allie licked and kissed, trailing fire along the way. Her breathing was shallow and she shuddered as she felt Allie nip and then taste her earlobe. Quinn’s legs began to buckle as waves of desire washed over her.

“Oh, God,” she groaned. It felt so good, but this was all happening too fast. Quinn pulled away from the kiss, her breathing ragged. Allie stared back at her, panting.

“I…Quinn—”

“No, it’s okay,” Quinn interrupted, her cheeks flushing. “I just need a little time to process.”

“I understand.” Allie smiled and then nodded down at the pink t-shirt that now seemed to be sculpted to Quinn’s body. “There’s a fairly large mall not too far from here. I saw it on the way back from the hospital the other night. What do you say we borrow Marge’s car and go get you something decent to wear?”

Chapter Fourteen

"You're kidding me, right?"

"Christ, Allie. What's wrong with this one?"

Allie stared at the light blue polo shirt Quinn held up in the air and tried to repress a shudder. From the look on the other woman's face, she knew that she had not quite succeeded.

"Other than the fact that it's a polo shirt? A powder blue polo shirt? A god-awfully ugly powder blue polo shirt?"

Quinn twisted her lips and glowered at Allie before hanging the shirt back on the rack. She looked around the clothing store and waved her hands in the air.

"I give up then. There's just nothing here that's going to work."

Seriously? Allie looked around at the row after row of women's clothing surrounding them and shook her head. The store was massive—she imagined that it was easily four times the size of her boutique in Marietta.

"Quinn, this place is huge. Look around you. I see several things that would be perfect for you."

"Such as?"

Allie stepped to her left and pointed to a rack of evening dresses.

"Well, right here. You would look stunning in this. Jessica Howard, three-quarter sleeve ruched lace. What do you think?"

The expression on Quinn's face spoke for her.

Not to be deterred, Allie continued on to another rack. She picked up a gray dress and held it up in front of Quinn. "All right, then. What about this? It's Calvin Klein. A very simple, but still gorgeous, sweater dress. We could pair it with a cute belt. I see some silver jewelry over there that would go nicely with it."

Quinn stared back at her from over the dress, midnight blue eyes flashing.

"Allie, I don't *do* dresses."

Allie narrowed her eyes, regarding Quinn sharply for a moment before returning the dress. There were few things in the world that Allie enjoyed as much as shopping, more so for other people than herself. Hell, shopping was what she did for a living, and she would be damned if they were going to leave the department store without at least one suitable outfit for Quinn.

"Quinn," she said, a thought suddenly occurring to her. "If you don't think you can't wear a dress because of…" Allie's voice trailed off as she motioned to Quinn's leg.

"Don't," Quinn warned in a low tone.

Allie knew that she had struck a nerve, but she wasn't going to let it go. She took a step forward and lightly ran her fingers down the length of one of Quinn's arms.

"No, I'm not going to let you do that. I've seen your legs—both of them—and they are a part of who you are." She grasped Quinn's hand and leveled a gaze at her. "And you are a very beautiful woman."

Quinn chewed on her bottom lip and stared back at Allie. She flexed, but rather than pull away as Allie expected, Quinn wrapped her fingers tightly around Allie's hand and drew her in close. Quinn's voice was a hot breath against Allie's ear as she whispered, causing Allie's stomach to give a little flutter.

"I don't do dresses."

Quinn dropped Allie's hand and brushed past her.

"Quinn…" Allie said turning, surprised to find that she was somewhat breathless.

The other woman threw a hand up and shook her head.

"Don't. I have not, nor will I ever be, a dress person." She leaned her back against one of the broad white columns that littered the store and seemed to shift her weight to her right side. Allie wondered if the bad leg was bothering her and mentally kicked herself for not considering whether or not Quinn had any problems standing on it for long periods of time. They'd been walking around the mall for well over an hour. She was about to suggest they take a break from shopping for a while when Quinn continued. "I'm not like you, Allie. You—you're all feminine and curvy. I'm just not."

"Look why—" *Wait, what*? "Curvy? What do you mean, I'm *curvy*?" Allie had been around the fashion industry long enough to know what 'curvy' was code for.

Quinn let out a laugh and shook her head.

"I didn't mean it like that," she said with a smile, her eyes dancing. "What I meant was, you're…you know. Voluptuous. You have the kind of body that was made to wear Calvin Klein and Jessica Tandy."

"Jessica Howard," Allie corrected with a grin.

"Whatever," Quinn said, pushing off the column. "Can we just find something and get out of here? I'm starting to get a little hungry, to tell you the truth."

Allie darted her eyes around the store and then motioned for Quinn to follow, leading her away from the dresses. "Of course. I see some black slacks that should cater to your tastes right over here. Everything goes with black. I'm sure we can find a suitable blouse to wear with them. Preferably something that is *not* a polyester blend."

"That's fine."

Allie thought about Quinn's words as they walked.

"Voluptuous, hmm?" she asked, trying to sound nonchalant.

"Mmhmm."

"That's an awfully big word."

"So it is."

Allie frowned, wondering if she was imagining things, or was Quinn edging closer to her as they walked?

"Army teach you words like that?"

"No ma'am. That word is brought to you by the letter 'V' and the outstanding teaching staff at the Georgia Institute of Technology."

She felt Quinn's fingers brush lightly against hers as they walked. A tiny shiver ran up Allie's arm, stirring a warmth in her chest.

"Oh, that's right," Allie said, stopping in front of a rack of black trousers. "I'd almost forgotten that you said you were a Georgia Tech graduate." She pushed the hangers around on the rack until she found the size she imagined would fit Quinn. Allie took the pants off the rack and moved to pass them to Quinn. It was definitely not her imagination when Quinn reached out as if to take the hanger, but instead overshot and seized Allie by the wrist. She began to rub tiny circles on the soft part of Allie's wrist with her thumb, mimicking Allie's action from earlier.

"You know, I have no idea where you went to college," Quinn said softly. "Or if you even went to college. In fact, there are several things about you that I'd like to know." Allie swallowed and was about to speak when Quinn placed two fingers to Allie's lips. "Nope, not yet. That will be one of my questions."

Allie playfully swiped away Quinn's hand and then cocked her head.

"Your questions? What are you talking about?"

Quinn shot Allie a sly smile and shook her head. "You'll see later." She took the hanger from Allie's hand and began to move towards the dressing room. "Let me go try these on. You go pick out a blouse for me to wear—no ruffles and for God's sakes no sequins. We can stop by that pizza place near where we parked to get something to go and then head back to the lodge to eat. You and I—Miss Alison Jenkins—are going to play a game."

"What are you talking about? What kind of a game?"

Quinn simply smiled and walked away, leaving Allie to ponder the other woman's words and wonder what the hell she had gotten herself into.

Chapter Fifteen

"So, I get five questions."

"Yes. Are there any napkins in that kitchen? This is greasier than I thought it would be."

"I don't think there are any napkins, but I know there's a roll of paper towels. You sit, I'll go get it."

Quinn pulled a slice of pepperoni pizza out of the large square box that sat on the coffee table as Allie strode into the kitchenette.

"God, this looks so good," she breathed, licking her lips in anticipation. Quinn didn't remember eating breakfast and was certain that she hadn't had anything for lunch, so was just this side of starving. The large pizza with pepperoni and extra cheese looked—and smelled—like heaven.

Allie sat back down on the other end of the couch and tossed Quinn the roll of paper towels.

"Don't make yourself sick eating that," she said as Quinn took a large bite of the pizza. "Any five questions?"

Quinn chased down the bite with a sip from the Diet Coke can sitting beside the pizza box and nodded. "I won't. And yes, any five questions. No question is off the table and all questions must be answered truthfully and to their fullest extent."

Allie reached into the box and took out a slice of pizza, shaking her head.

"I have to say this is the craziest game I've heard of."

Quinn shrugged. "One of the lieutenants in the unit invented it as a quick and easy way to get to know new people." Quinn took a bite and then grinned as a thought struck her. "Of course," she added, "he came up with it after watching *Silence of the Lambs* and our version usually involved a shot of tequila in between questions."

"Oh Lord, '*Quid pro quo*, Clarice'?"

"Exactly," Quinn said laughing. "I'll get us started. Where did you go to college?"

"Well, while my father wanted me to keep the family tradition going by attending the University of Georgia, I did not—"

"I knew there was something I liked about you," Quinn interjected in between bites.

"Whatever. Anyway, I didn't go to Georgia like Dad wanted me to. Instead, I attended Georgia State University where I majored in business."

"Really? Just down the road from Tech." Quinn tore off a paper towel and wiped the grease from her fingers. "I went out with a girl from Georgia State for a while," she said wistfully as she remembered the blonde education major with legs that went on forever, and then shook her head. “That bitch was crazy. When we broke up, she kept all my Tori Amos CDs.”

Allie laughed and reached for her drink.

“Okay, my turn. What’s your cat’s name?”

“Cat.”

“Your cat’s name is not ‘cat’, come on.”

“Well, technically it’s not my cat. And yes, that’s what I call it—Cat.”

Allie raised one eyebrow. “Well, whose cat is it, then? It sure seemed like your cat the day I was at your house.”

“It’s Laurie’s cat.” Quinn felt a tightness in her chest and realized that she hadn’t actually spoken her ex-girlfriend’s name aloud for months.

“Who is Laurie?” Allie asked.

Quinn shook her head. “Nope, that’s a separate question. You’ll have to use one of your other turns.” She looked away from Allie and took another sip of Diet Coke. Thoughts of Laurie were definitely not what she had on the agenda for this evening.

“All right, that’s fair enough.”

“Next question,” Quinn said. “How old where you when you first kissed a girl in public?”

Allie thought for a moment and then smiled.

"When I *first* kissed a girl, or when I first *kissed* a girl?"

Quinn eased back into the couch and drew her legs up under her. "Let me get comfortable for this one," she said, smirking. "The rules say you must answer the question to its fullest extent."

"Okay, then. When I *first* kissed a girl was in high school. I was in the band and we had taken a trip to Disney World. Everyone was riding the Pirates of the Caribbean. Me and my friend Angie were the only ones not on the ride with their boyfriend. Everyone else was making out, so as a joke we did too."

"Was she hot?" Quinn asked.

"Is that one of your questions?"

"All right, never mind. Go on."

"The first time I *kissed* a girl was on the fourth of July. I was twenty-three and had been out for a few months. Her name was Austin—like the city—and she *was* hot. We had gone to Stone Mountain Park with a group of friends and made out on a blanket during the fireworks."

"Sounds like one hell of a fireworks show."

Quinn smiled as she saw Allie blush. Just when she thought Allie couldn't get any more appealing, she did little things like that.

"My turn again," Allie said. "Why the Army?"

Quinn was surprised, thinking that Allie would have returned to the 'Laurie question'. She reached back to get another slice of pizza.

"That's an easy one. The Army helped pay for school. A large part of my tuition was paid for by a ROTC scholarship, which especially came in handy after my junior year when I came out to my parents, and they stopped talking to me. Of course, I wasn't out to the world—don't ask, don't tell and all. Nine-eleven was still fresh around that time and the Army was expanding fast. I more or less fell into the chance to fly helicopters for Uncle Sam and never looked back."

Quinn took another sip of her drink as she eyed Allie. It was impossible to gauge what the other woman was thinking.

"I guess it's funny how different our parents seem to be," Allie finally said.

Quinn shrugged. "I came to peace with that a long time ago. My turn now. What's the longest relationship you've ever had?"

Allie ran a hand through her hair as she thought about her answer.

"Has to be Corey Stevens. We started dating in high school—he was my date to the Junior Prom—and didn't break up until my sophomore year of college. He's actually the reason I went to Georgia State. Well, one of them, anyway. After Corey, there were guys, and then girls, here and there. Austin and I dated for about a year. There were a few women after her, but no one really serious. Then Amanda and I decided to go into business together, and I didn't have time to date, or at least so I thought. I blinked and four years went by. The boutiques were running on their own, and I suddenly had all the time in the world and no one to spend it with. Then one day this really hot Army chick comes into my store with her slightly crazy little sister."

Quinn couldn't help but laugh at that last. She looked at Allie sitting beside her on the couch and thought that chilly Saturday morning in March felt like a lifetime ago.

"Crazy little sister is right," she muttered.

"Okay," Allie said. "Who is Laurie?"

Quinn was momentarily taken aback by the question, even though she was expecting it. Outside of Rebekah, she'd never really talked about the break-up with Laurie. It was strange, but she felt like she needed to and she needed to do it with the woman sitting across from her.

"I've only ever had two really serious relationships—and no, Crazy GSU Bitch was not one of them." Quinn placed the half-eaten slice of pizza she'd been nibbling on back into the box and then sat back on the couch. "I met Laurie a few years ago. Erin had just had her youngest about the same time I had leave, so I decided to come home for a visit."

"Who is Erin?"

"My older sister."

"Oh," Allie said. "I didn't realize you had another sister. I thought it was just Rebekah."

"No, Erin is the oldest," Quinn said and then gave a derisive snort. "She's the child my mother always wished I would be. Married to a nice, boring guy. Three kids, two dogs, PTO chairperson. I'll just say we don't see eye to eye on a lot of things and leave it at that."

"I understand."

"So, I met Laurie while I was home and we hit it off. That was just before this last deployment."

"Oh."

Quinn watched Allie as she continued. "Yeah. It was actually good for a while. The long distance relationship was working out. She met me in Italy during a two-week leave and we bummed around Rome. I'll be honest. I was in love." Allie stared back her, but Quinn couldn't get a feel for what she was thinking. She realized her throat was dry and took the last swallow of the Diet Coke.

"I take it she wasn't?" Allie asked quietly.

Quinn twisted her lips.

"I don't know. I thought she was, too. Then the crash happened. Everything after was more or less a blur. A lot of surgeries. A lot of time in the hospital. Physical therapy. Hell, I'm still doing PT. I guess it was a lot to ask someone to deal with."

"Pardon my French, Quinn, but that's bullshit."

Quinn started at Allie's interruption.

"What?"

"You heard me. She knew exactly what she was signing up for when she started a relationship with someone in the Army. A relationship with anyone. So what, she couldn't handle it when you got hurt? What if it had been a car wreck instead of a helicopter crash? What would she have done then?"

"I don't know, I never thought about it that way."

"Well, if you ask me, you're better off without her. She sounds like a shallow bitch."

Quinn grinned. "Rebekah calls her a skank."

"I can't disagree."

Quinn sighed and rubbed the back of her neck with one hand. "So, that's Laurie," she said and then stood. "If you don't mind, I need to use the restroom."

"I told you all that pizza was going to make you sick," Allie scolded.

Quinn chuckled as she made her way towards the bedroom.

"Watch it," she said. "You're going to start sounding like your Aunt Marge."

Quinn ignored Allie's retort as she closed the bedroom door behind her and walked into the bathroom. She stood in front of the sink and stared at her reflection in the mirror. She closed her eyes and exhaled. It was a cliché, but she did feel like a weight had been lifted. It suddenly occurred to her that she couldn't quite picture Laurie's face anymore. Not exactly. Not the details, anyway. It was all more or less impressions, and bad ones at that. Quinn opened her eyes and looked back at herself in the mirror. She could, however, picture in great detail the good-looking woman who was currently sitting on the couch in the living room. The one with the pouty pink lips and golden brown hair. The woman who had called her beautiful and whose kiss made Quinn's knees weak.

Quinn turned on the sink and washed her hands and then splashed water on her face. She grabbed a towel hanging from the rack on the wall and then turned away from the mirror, stepping out of the bathroom and moving back towards the living room. She knew what—and who—she wanted. Now, to find a way not to fuck it up.

Chapter Sixteen

Allie slid onto the barstool next to Quinn and grimaced at the wet, sticky substance on the tall, black table in front of her. She couldn't help but stare at it, and was just about to suggest to Quinn they switch tables when a red-headed waitress with incredibly large breasts walked up and wiped it away with a dingy white towel.

"Evening ladies," the waitress drawled. "What'll it be tonight?"

"Whatever light beer you have on tap is fine," Allie heard Quinn say.

"Sure thing. And you honey?" The waitress asked, looking directly at Allie.

"I don't suppose you have any white wine, do you?" The look on the waitress's face told her that wine—white or any other color—was not something to be found at Duke's Bar and Grill. "Do you have anything frozen, then? Daiquiri or a margarita?"

"Yup. So one light beer and one frozen margarita. Do you want anything to eat with that? Chicken wings or cheese sticks?"

"No thank you."

Allie glanced over at Quinn as the waitress turned and made her way back to the bar. Quinn was holding back a laugh.

"Is there something you want to say?" Allie inquired.

"You don't go to many bars, do you?" the other woman answered with a grin.

"Oh, shut up. I still can't believe I let you talk me into this."

"C'mon now, Allie. When your sister shows up on the night before her wedding and says that she needs to go out, you go. Even I know that."

Allie cast a glance at Quinn and sighed. While she knew Quinn was right, sitting in a sketchy, smoke-filled bar was still the last place she wanted to be right now. When her sister showed up at the room an hour or so ago, Allie was more than ready to decline the offer of tagging along with Taylor and the other bridesmaids to the bar down the street from the lodge. Quinn, however, had surprised Allie and said yes before Allie had the chance to get a word in edgewise. Allie wondered if the conversation about Laurie had more than a little to do with Quinn's insistence that they go.

"Oh, look. I think Taylor is about to sing karaoke," Quinn said, pointing across the small wooden dance floor that sat to their left.

Allie groaned when she saw Taylor and two of her college roommates flipping through the karaoke book, giggling as they went through the song list.

God, please not karaoke.

“I say again, I can’t believe I let you talk me into this,” Allie groaned and rubbed her eyes. “I really, really hate karaoke.”

“Here you go ladies,” the waitress interrupted, placing their drinks down on the table. “If you need anything else, you just let me know.”

“Okay, thank you,” Allie said, staring at the extraordinarily large glass overflowing with the bright green frozen margarita.

“There’s no way those are real,” Quinn said in a low voice.

“What?”

“The waitress. There’s no way those are real,” she said, picking up the beer and taking a sip.

“I can’t believe you just said that.” Allie took a small drink of the margarita and then coughed sharply. “Oh my God, that is strong.”

Beside her, Quinn shrugged. “I call them like I see them.”

Allie turned on the barstool to face Quinn. She opened her mouth to speak, but then forgot what she was going to say when Quinn winked at her.

"So, do you make it a habit to check out waitresses?" she asked, finally gathering her thoughts.

Quinn smiled. "Is that one of your questions?"

"Oh, are we still playing?"

"Of course. We haven't gotten to five questions yet," Quinn said, swirling the beer around in her glass. "Unless you'd rather stop at three. I think that's where we were when Taylor interrupted."

Allie shook her head.

"No, we can keep going." She sipped the margarita, wincing as the alcohol burned her throat. "All right, then. Do you make it a habit to check out waitresses?"

Quinn grinned and then winked at her again.

"As a general rule, no. However, when presented with an absurdly large set of man-made boobies, I will acknowledge their existence." Quinn reached out and ran her fingers alongside Allie's chest. "On a more personal note, I am partial to the real things. They just feel better and are generally more…responsive." Allie shivered as Quinn began to lightly caress the edge of one breast. "Size doesn't really matter, although you certainly can't go wrong with a nice c-cup."

Allie's mouth went dry when she saw the other woman staring back at her with a penetrating look in her dark blue eyes. She'd seen similar flashes of intensity from Quinn in the past. That day at her house when they'd argued, then later at The Varsity with that man. But that had been different. On those occasions Quinn had been angry, aggressive, commanding. This was different. This was sexual, powerful, almost predatory. *And fucking hot.*

Before Allie could respond she heard her sister's voice begin to belt out a very bad rendition of a Garth Brooks song.

"Lord," she groaned and took another sip of the margarita. She looked back to Quinn and smiled as the auburn haired woman winked at her again. "Why do you keep winking at me?" Allie asked with a smirk.

Quinn frowned and sat back on the barstool.

"What?"

"You keep winking at me. Not that I mind, but…"

Quinn bit her bottom lip and shook her head before running a hand over her eyes.

"I'm sorry. It wasn't intentional."

Not intentional?

"How do you accidentally wink at someone Quinn?"

"It's…I wasn't winking like you think," she said and took a draw on the beer. "It's my right eye. The retina partially detached in the crash. They did surgery and repaired most of the damage, but I don't see well at night out of it. It's dark in here, so my vision on that side is a little blurry right now. It's just my eye trying to adjust."

"Oh," Allie said, dropping her gaze to the table, suddenly feeling uncomfortable. "I'm sorry, I shouldn't have said anything."

Quinn put a hand on Allie's leg and squeezed.

"Hey, it's okay."

Allie looked back up at Quinn and smiled. "All right. I guess I need to choose my next question wisely. I only have one left."

Quinn sat back on the barstool and took a sip of the beer.

"So you do. Let's see…my turn." She winced as Taylor hit a high note—badly—and then folded her arms. "Okay, I got it. Why Mimi's?"

Allie choked down another sip of the margarita before answering.

"Why *Mimi's* or *why* Mimi's? Do you want to know about the name or why I went into business with Amanda?"

"Answer the question to its fullest extent."

Allie narrowed her eyes at Quinn and shook her head.

"You keep asking these questions with multiple answers. I feel like you're cheating somehow."

Quinn shrugged and then said, "Well, I have played this game a time or two before. So…"

"All right, then. I—"

"Allie, you and Quinn are not going to just sit here all night. We are here to have some fun," Taylor suddenly interrupted, plopping down on the barstool across from Allie.

"Taylor, I think you're drunk," Allie said sharply to her sister.

"Allie, I know I'm drunk. C'mon, Tina and Sherri are getting us a table." Not waiting for an answer, Taylor jumped up from the table and bounded to the far side of the bar. Allie could see the other bridesmaids laughing and talking to two young men in cowboy hats next to a pool table in the small room off from the bar.

Hell no, Allie thought. She was just about to say as much to Quinn when the slender woman suddenly slid off the barstool and grabbed Allie by the arm.

"What do you think you're doing?" Allie challenged.

"We're going to play pool," she answered, her eyes dancing.

"Have you lost your mind?"

Allie tried to pull away, but Quinn tightened her grip on Allie's arm and took a step closer. She leaned in, so close that her cheek almost brushed Allie's.

"Do you know how many times over the past year I've had the chance—or would have wanted to if I had—to go spend time with a drop-dead gorgeous woman at a bar? Even if it is some redneck country western bar in the middle of nowhere North Carolina?" Quinn's eyes were serious as she regarded Allie. "I know this is not your kinda place. Hell, it's not mine either, but—"

"Okay, we can go play pool," Allie interjected with a defeated sigh.

"Awesome." Quinn stepped back and waved to Taylor, who was shouting their name from across the bar. "One minute," she called back.

"You know, I haven't played pool since I was in college," Allie said. Looking at Quinn, she was surprised by how different the woman seemed. She wasn't sure what had spurred this sudden change in personality, but she wasn't going to complain about it.

"I've played here and there. And, we've already established that I like a tight rack," Quinn said, flashing a grin as Allie swatted a hand at her. "Don't worry, your sister and her friends don't strike me as pool sharks."

Allie glanced over at the trio of cackling women. "I think you're right on that account." She picked up her drink and stood, and then reached out to grasp Quinn's arms as she felt the world start to spin.

"Are you okay?"

"Whew. I am. I think that drink is a little too strong."

Allie felt her heart skip a beat when Quinn wrapped an arm around Allie's waist to steady her. She looked up at Quinn and then lightly touched her on the cheek, as if to wipe away the concerned frown that was there.

"Maybe we should skip pool, then." Quinn said.

"No, I'm fine," Allie insisted, finally finding her feet. "C'mon, let's go have some fun."

Chapter Seventeen

"Okay, Allie, just about here. Let me get the key out."

Quinn pushed her hip against Allie—a very drunk Allie—pinning her against the hallway wall as Quinn fished in her back pocket for the room key. Quinn slid the keycard in the lock and then kicked the door open with one foot, dragging Allie into the hotel room with her.

"I told you I can walk Quinn," Allie said, her words slurring together.

"Yeah, that's why I've had to pick you up off the ground three times between here and the elevator," Quinn muttered. She walked Allie into the bedroom and dumped her onto the king-sized bed that sat in the corner of the room. Allie landed on her stomach with a soft moan and then rolled over onto her back. Quinn sat down beside her and began to unlace her own shoes, kicking them off into the corner.

"How's your hand?" Allie murmured from her prone position.

Quinn held her right hand out in front of her, wincing as she flexed her fingers. Two of the knuckles were swollen and beginning to turn a faint shade of purple.

"Hurts like a motherfucker, Allie," she responded tersely. Quinn didn't think they were broken, though. She rose from the bed with a sigh and walked into the bathroom to run cold water over them.

"If it makes you feel any better, I think you broke that cowboy's nose when you hit him."

Quinn swore as the cold water hit her swollen knuckles. "Not really, to tell you the truth," she called back to the bedroom. "Served him right for putting his hand up my shirt, though." She flexed her fingers again and then turned off the water. Quinn grabbed one of the towels hanging by the sink and walked back into the bedroom, drying her hands.

"Well, you did keep winking at him," Allie pointed out as she sat up on the bed.

"Goddamn, how many times do I have say that I wasn't winking," Quinn hissed as she passed by the bed and headed into the kitchenette area. She opened the freezer door and pulled out the small, blue ice tray, and then walked to the sink with it. Quinn dumped the ice into the sink and then picked up three of the cubes, wrapping them in the bath towel. "And even if I had been," she continued, moving back into the bedroom, "that still didn't give him the right to put his hand up my shirt."

"I know," Allie said and then cocked her head. "Are you limping?"

"Yes, I'm limping," Quinn grumbled, sitting back on the bed. She gingerly placed the towel-covered ice over her knuckles.

"No…I mean, are you limping on your other leg?"

Quinn looked over to Allie and let out a breath.

"Yes, Allie. I'm limping on my other leg. Your sister's friend Tina got me in the knee when she reared back to kick the other cowboy in the balls."

"Oh," Allie said and began to bite her quivering bottom lip.

In all the time she'd spent in the Army, Quinn had seen more than her fair share of drunks. It was inevitable that when soldiers—both officers and enlisted—found themselves on leave and at an establishment that sold alcohol, at least some of them would overdo it. There were the fighting drunks, the happy drunks, and the drunks who simply got sick and then passed out. Allie, Quinn had discovered, was the worst type of drunk.

"I'm so sorry, Quinn," Allie wailed.

She was a crying drunk.

"Goddamn it, Allie. We agreed no more crying, remember?" Quinn warned.

Allie nodded, wiping the tears from her eyes. She mumbled something that Quinn couldn't make out and fell back onto the bed, curling up on her side. She was asleep almost immediately, making a little snoring noise that Quinn found to be unbelievably sexy.

Cursing, Quinn stood from the bed and walked to the side where Allie lay. She hooked her hands under Allie's shoulders and pulled her effortlessly up to the pillow. Quinn tugged off Allie's shoes and let them drop to the floor by the bed. She drew the sheet up over the sleeping woman and then turned to switch off the bedroom light. Quinn shucked off her shirt and pants and then laid them neatly on the dresser. She eased across the bed and crawled under the covers, sighing as her head hit the cool pillow.

What a hell of a day.

Quinn closed her eyes and willed her tired muscles to relax. She couldn't remember the last time she'd been involved in a good bar fight. Had to have been at that little pub in the airport in Shannon, Ireland, on the way back from the first tour in Afghanistan. Regardless, while tonight had been fun in a perverse sort of way, it was certainly not how she imagined the evening with Allie ending.

Quinn had almost dozed completely off when she suddenly felt the lightest of touches on her arm. She opened her eyes and lay still, wondering if she imagined it, when she felt it again.

There was no mistaking what—or who—it was.

"Allie…" Quinn began, turning to face the other woman.

"Hey," Allie said, staring back at her with glassy eyes.

"Hey."

"What are you doing?"

Quinn groaned.

"Allie, honey, it's time to go to sleep."

Allie smiled and reached one arm out from under the sheet, softly caressing the side of Quinn's cheek.

"I'm not sleepy. Are you?"

Quinn sighed. *Lord.*

"Yes, actually I am. And you're drunk. C'mon, let's go to sleep."

Despite her hopes, Allie was not going along with Quinn's suggestion. Allie shifted in the bed, slowly easing her way forward. Quinn swallowed as Allie's warm skin touched her own, Allie's naked breasts pressing softly against her chest. A thought suddenly occurred to Quinn.

"Allie, what happened to your clothes?"

She was met with a lazy smile.

"What do you think happened to them?" Allie bent her head and slid her hand up into Quinn's hair, wrapping it around her fingers. Quinn moaned as she felt first Allie's lips and then her tongue begin to probe her own. The kiss deepened, Allie drawing in Quinn's lower lip and lightly brushing against it with her teeth. Quinn arched her back as she felt Allie's fingers begin to roam down her ribcage, slowly running along the line of Quinn's bra. When she felt Allie's fingers begin to play with the latch, she groaned and pulled away.

"No," she panted, grasping both of Allie's hands in her own.

"Quinn…" Allie pleaded. "I want you so much it hurts."

"No, Allie," Quinn said. "Not tonight, not after you've had too much to drink." She moved closer and rolled Allie back on her side, pressing closely to her from behind. *I deserve a fucking medal for this,* she thought as she wrapped one arm around Allie's waist, the other just touching the top of Allie's head.

Allie shifted restlessly in her arms.

"Quinn," she protested. "Please."

Quinn dipped her head and nuzzled the soft of Allie's neck.

"Shh," she whispered. "Sleep." She began to gently stroke Allie's stomach, relishing the feel of Allie's delicate flesh beneath her fingers. After a few minutes she felt Allie's breathing begin to even out and then heard the other woman's soft snoring begin again. Quinn continued to hold

Allie, tightening the embrace as she felt her own body relax and sleep overtake her.

Chapter Eighteen

"Rebekah, I swear to God, if you let that woman in my house, I will not be responsible for my actions."

Allie pretended not to listen to the telephone conversation between Quinn and her sister. Quinn was sitting on the black leather couch in the living room of the hotel suite, her legs curled up under her, one hand covering her eyes.

"Allie said she asked you to feed the cat. That is all. There's no reason for you to bring Mom over there," Quinn said into the phone. "What? No. Are you kidding me? Clean what? There's nothing to be cleaned."

Allie smiled discreetly and turned back towards the kitchenette area, where her Aunt Marge was busy chopping fruit.

"Aunt Marge, I still don't understand why you're doing this," she said, as the elderly woman chopped a strawberry into quarters.

"After what happened to your poor little lesbian friend Quinn, I'm not eating anything that comes out of that kitchen tonight."

"Would you stop calling her that," Allie instructed. "And you're being ridiculous. The food will be perfectly fine."

“Well, that’s not a chance I’m willing to take. If I got sick like that at my age it would kill me,” Aunt Marge pronounced.

Allie shook her head as she watched her aunt begin to cut through a cantaloupe like a ninja.

“I don’t give a damn if she’s just *trying to be helpful* or not, keep her out. How hard is it, Rebekah? Just tell her no. What? What do you mean she’s there now?”

“Aunt Marge, can’t you do this in your room?” Allie asked.

The older woman shook her head. “Nope. Your uncle went fishing with Alan early this morning and there’s fish guts everywhere. Have you ever heard of such a thing? Who goes fishing during a wedding then brings the nasty things back to the room for cleaning?”

“We *are* at a lodge, Aunt Marge.”

Aunt Marge made a tutting sound as she shook her head and then chopped a grape in half. “At a lodge. That’s the most ridiculous thing I’ve ever heard. You’re as bad as they are.”

“Why is she in the refrigerator? I’ve been gone two days, the milk is not going to go bad before I get home.”

"Don't they make fruit trays already prepared? Why didn't you get one of those instead of going to all this trouble?"

"What trouble? It's cutting up grapes, how is that trouble? And do you know how much they wanted for one of those fruit trays? Eleven dollars and ninety-nine cents!"

Allie sighed and shook her head, thinking to herself that her aunt had probably spent twice that amount buying the individual fruit.

"My bedroom? Rebekah, you keep her out of my bedroom. Because. Because, that's why. What? No. I have *things* in there Rebekah, things that she does not need to see. *Things.* Do you understand what I'm saying? Well do it now. I'm hanging up, Rebekah."

Allie heard Quinn disconnect the call, stand up from the couch and then walk to the kitchenette bar.

"So," Allie said, flashing a grin at the woman. "How are things at home?"

"Don't start," Quinn muttered as she sat on the barstool next to Allie's. She cocked an eye as Marge began to peel an apple. "Aunt Marge, what are you doing?"

Aunt Marge looked up from the cutting board at Quinn and went through the whole spiel again. Allie was resisting the urge to roll her eyes listening to the story a second time when she suddenly felt something lightly rubbing against her leg. She glanced down to see Quinn's leg sliding up and down against her own.

Well, now.

"Are you kidding? Twelve dollars for some fruit? That's highway robbery," Quinn said sympathetically and then eased off the barstool. "Well, I hate to be bad company, but I really need to go get dressed for the day."

"Well, you take care, honey," Aunt Marge called as Quinn shuffled out of the room, closing the bedroom door behind her. As soon as the door closed, Aunt Marge put the knife down and looked at Allie. "So, she's a lovely young woman."

Oh, brother.

"Yes, she is," Allie replied.

"It's a shame about her face, though," Aunt Marge said as she began to slide the cut fruit into an empty plastic bowl.

"Aunt Marge," Allie seethed. "Please."

Allie jumped, she wasn't sure if was because her phone suddenly began to flash and vibrate, or that she was afraid that Quinn would hear her aunt.

"What?" the older woman said with a shrug. "I'm just saying."

"Well, say it somewhere else," she snapped, picking up her phone.

She frowned. It was a text message from Quinn. *I'm going to take a shower.*

"All I mean is that they have doctors for things like that," Aunt Marge continued, wetting a paper towel from the sink area and walking back to bar. "My Cousin Vivian had the same thing happen to her. She went to that doctor in Nashville and he took care of it right there in the office. She was in and out in two hours. There's no reason that your little lesbian friend couldn't do the same."

Wait, what?

"Aunt Marge, what are you talking about?"

Allie eyed the woman as she wiped down the countertop with the paper towel.

"Her nose, Allie. She would be so pretty if it wasn't for that nose. When Vivian broke hers—one of those kids of hers was playing ball in the house and hit her in the face—she had her nose fixed and you'd never know the difference."

She stared incredulously at her aunt. She glanced down as she felt her phone vibrate again. It was another text from Quinn. *Getting in now. Room for two.*

Allie read the message a second time and then looked back up at her aunt.

"Aunt Marge, it's time go." Allie stood from the barstool and quickly walked into the kitchenette.

"What? What do you mean it's time go? What about the fruit?"

Allie grabbed the plastic bowl from the bar and placed it in the refrigerator.

"Fruit's done, Aunt Marge." She grabbed the woman by the arm and led her to the front door. "I just remembered I have to make an important call for work. Why don't you go see if Taylor needs any help with her dress?" She asked, all put pushing the woman out the door and closing—and locking it—behind her.

Allie began to move towards the bedroom. She had just placed a hand on the doorknob when she heard the sound of water running. She swallowed, her hands suddenly too sweaty to turn the knob.

Taking a calming breath, she opened the door and stepped inside the room. The bathroom door was cracked, the sound of the running shower echoing through the bedroom. As Allie reached the door, it opened the rest of the way. Her breath caught as she saw Quinn standing in front of her, beautifully naked. Allie could only stare and, as if in a trance, accept the outstretched hand that Quinn offered. She could feel heat tickling across her stomach as Quinn drew her in close, steam spilling out from the shower into the bathroom.

"I think," Quinn said, her tone low and seductive, "that you have far too many clothes on." Quinn held Allie's eyes as she spoke, her fingers slipping open the buttons on Allie's shirt. At the last one, she slipped the shirt from her and then leaned forward, her lips falling onto the edge of Allie's shoulder as the blouse dropped to the ground. Allie drew in a breath as she felt Quinn's tongue skim across her collarbone. Quinn's fingers dipped into the waistband of Allie's shorts at the same time she began to softly suckle at the base of her neck. Allie moaned and began to stir restlessly under the gentle suction.

Quinn stepped back towards the shower and pulled Allie in with her. Allie shivered as the warm water fell across her exposed skin, streaming down her back and sides in a massaging rhythm. Quinn smiled and wound her arms around Allie's waist, stepping forward to embrace her, pressing their bodies together. Allie let her head fall back into the cascading water, her eyes closing as her lips parted in silent invitation. Allie moaned as she felt Quinn's tongue sweep across the inside of her lower lip, kissing her deeply, softly, thoroughly. Passion built deep in Allie's core, spilling out and spreading across her body until nothing existed but the pulse of the water against her back and the taste of Quinn's mouth against her own.

Allie felt herself turning, Quinn's warm body molding to her back.

"Quinn," she moaned as Quinn began to nuzzle the soft part of her neck. Licking, lapping the water collected there. Allie whimpered as she realized Quinn now had full access to her breasts. She leaned into Quinn, the other woman's diamond hard nipples a hot brand across her back. Quinn cupped Allie's breasts, circling her thumbs lightly around her erect nipples, pinching, setting every nerve in Allie's body on fire. Allie trembled as Quinn's hands slowly slid down, tracing the outline of Allie's hips, lightly touching her mound, pushing between her folds. Allie moaned as she felt soft fingers brush over her clit in slow, circular strokes. Tiny sparks of electricity shook her as she felt Quinn's tongue lick up along her neck, teeth lightly nibbling at her earlobe. Quinn began to mimic the motion of her fingers with her tongue, licking and sucking Allie's ear in tandem with her intimate caress. When she felt Quinn glide two fingers into her, Allie shattered, falling back onto Quinn's body as the climax took her, quivering and screaming Quinn's name.

Chapter Nineteen

"Are you sure you don't want any of the roast beef, Quinn?"

Quinn smiled and shook her head at Allie's mother, an energetic sixty-something version of Allie's sister Taylor. A little heavier than Taylor, but with the same large, bouncy brown hair that looked like it had been styled by someone from a John Hughes film.

"No ma'am, I'm fine, thank you." After the tuna salad and last night's greasy pizza, Quinn had decided to keep her food options simple for the remainder of the weekend and was sticking to the rice pilaf and a small portion of green beans.

"Well, if you change your mind, it certainly is delicious."

"It oughta be, as much as this is whole thing is costing," Allie's father Alan grumbled, not quite under his breath.

Quinn grinned as she saw Allie's mother swat at her husband. The couple had a very easy going, almost playful relationship that she found endearing.

"I'll keep that in mind," Quinn replied and then took a sip of her ice water. She'd opted to avoid both the wine and the champagne that were free flowing in the reception hall since she would be flying in the morning.

"Well, I hate that you've had such a rough time of it this week. Although we certainly are grateful that you were able to bring Allie up here. It wouldn't have been the same without our Sugar Bug," Allie's mom said in between bites of roast beef.

Sugar Bug? That one she was definitely going to have fun with later.

"Oh my God Mom, are you kidding me?" Allie snapped from across the table.

"What?" the older woman asked in an only sweet voice.

"You know what. And leave Quinn alone, I'm sure she doesn't feel like answering questions all night."

"It's fine, Allie. I really don't mind."

"Well," Allie's mother said, sawing into another slice of roast beef, "I was just trying to make conversation. I understand if you're still feeling under the weather after the other day."

"No, I'm feeling much better, thank you. Allie and I went shopping yesterday so I'd have something decent to wear to the wedding, and then called it an early night." She felt rather than saw the sideways glance that Allie threw her from across the table

"Well, good," Allie's mother said and then waived at Aunt Marge and Uncle Barney as they walked by the table on their way to the dance floor.

"So, Quinn," Alan said, sitting back in his chair. "Allie tells us that you graduated from the North Atlanta Trade School."

Quinn nodded at the name she knew many rival University of Georgia graduates dubbed Georgia Tech. "I did. I take it you're a Bulldog man?"

"I am. You know," he bent over towards his wife, "I heard the Georgia Tech football team has to eat cereal straight from the box."

"And why is that dear?" she asked, not looking up from her plate.

"Because they choke whenever they get near a bowl," he said, chuckling at his own joke.

"That's funny, because I heard that at the Georgia games they had to stop putting ice in the drinks," Quinn grinned at him.

"Oh really? I don't think I've heard that."

"Well, they had to. The student who knew the recipe graduated."

“All right, that’s enough you two,” Allie chided as both Quinn and her father began to laugh loud enough to draw looks from nearby tables.

Quinn smiled at Allie and couldn’t help but think again how irresistible she looked in her bridesmaid dress. It was all white lace and pink satin, with tiny little crystals around the neckline, and Quinn wanted nothing more than to peel it off of her. *And I may just do that later tonight…*

Allie leaned back in her chair and stretched.

“You know, it’s been a long day and I’m really getting tired. I don’t suppose anyone would mind if I called it an early night, would they?” she asked, yawning. Quinn raised one eyebrow, wondering if Allie had perhaps found a way to read her mind.

“Of course not, dear,” Allie’s mother said. “But be sure to take some of that cake with you. It looks like there’s going to be a ton of it left over.”

“Lord, please. That cake cost more than my first car,” Allie’s father added.

“Alan, one more word about how much money you’ve spent…” his wife warned.

“I will Mom,” Allie said, rising from the table. “Quinn, don’t feel like you have to rush off. You’re welcome to stay and talk football all night.”

"No, that's okay," Quinn quickly rose from her chair. "I'm pretty beat myself. Thank you again for having me this weekend. It was a beautiful wedding," she said to Allie's parents as she moved to follow Allie, who was already heading across the dance floor towards the exit.

As they reached the door, Allie came to an abrupt stop. She twirled and almost ran into Quinn.

"Whoa," Quinn said with a grin.

"Sorry, I forgot the cake."

"Well, go on and get a slice. Or two. I'll wait here."

Allie smiled and gave her a quick peck on the forehead. "I'll be right back," she said. Quinn felt a warm feeling spread across her chest as she watched Allie hurry back across the dance floor to the dessert table. A sudden brush against her arm drew Quinn's attention. She turned her head to see the West Virginia cousins walking by.

"Excuse you," Quinn muttered under her breath, glaring at the women as they passed by without addressing Quinn directly, but speaking loud enough to each other so that she could hear what they said. *Bitche*s, Quinn thought, narrowing her eyes at them.

"What did she just say?" A sharp voice behind her made Quinn jump. Startled, Quinn glanced over to see Aunt Marge. What appeared to be a very pissed off Aunt Marge.

"Lord, you scared me there for a second."

"I'm sorry, dear. Now, what did she say?"

"What do who say?"

"Alan's inbred cousin over there," she said, motioning to the women who had just walked by. "I heard what she said, but surely I had to be mistaken."

Quinn twisted her lips and shook her head.

"Don't worry about it, Aunt Marge. It's nothing I haven't heard before. We're in the South." Quinn smiled and winked at the flustered woman. "Not everyone is as forward thinking as you are."

"Well, I don't care if we're on Mars, I'm not going to stand here and listen to anyone say those words in my presence."

"Marge, please," Quinn said, placing a hand on Aunt Marge's arm. "I don't want to cause a scene and embarrass Allie or her parents."

Aunt Marge patted Quinn's hand and then made a tutting sound.

"Don't you worry, honey. I won't cause a scene," she said with a gleam in her eye. "Now, you just stand back and let me give you a lesson in how to be a passive aggressive Southern bitch."

Chapter Twenty

"No, she did not say that!"

"Yes, she did," Quinn laughed as she walked through the door of the hotel room. "And then she started in on the other two. Did you know that your Cousin Jane is on her fourth husband?"

"I can't believe I missed it," Allie said, closing the door behind them and then placing the large plate of cake on the bar by the kitchenette.

"Aunt Marge is my hero." Quinn sat on the edge of the black leather couch and slid off her shoes. She curled her legs up on the couch, briefly massaging the ache in her left ankle, and then eased back into the cushion. "I almost hate to go home tomorrow and get back to the real world."

Allie moved away from the bar and sat beside Quinn on the couch. She leaned against the couch cushion and stared at Quinn, looking as if she was considering something.

"Quinn," she said finally, "I know we haven't talked about it, really, but I'd like this to continue when we get back home. I mean…I assume that this morning was not, you know…" Allie flushed as her voice trailed off.

Quinn eyed her for a moment and then smiled.

"I would like that, too," she answered quietly. "I've never had a problem with long distance relationships. Not that…what, you live in Woodstock, so that's like forty-five minutes, from my house?" Allie nodded. "So, you're not that far away. I know my current track record may not be all that great, but..." Her eyes went dark as she thought about Laurie.

A hand on her arm brought her out of her thoughts. Quinn looked up at Allie.

"Hey, I thought we agreed that you-know-who is a bitch. Oh, sorry…skank. Don't even think about her," Allie said softly. "And besides, you're not the Lone Ranger in the relationship department, remember? It's been so long that I had anyone that I was even remotely interested in, that I don't even want to think about it." Allie said thoughtfully. She smiled at Quinn. "Well, was so long, I should say."

Quinn grinned at her.

"So, Miss Jenkins, would you say that I am a prospect then?"

"Oh my God, I am so sick of hearing that word."

"Well then…" Quinn reached up and gripped Allie's hand to pull her in close. "…Sugar Bug…"

"I may literally kill my mother for that."

"Please, I think it's cute." Quinn lowered her eyes and breathed deeply, taking in Allie's scent. She smelled like peaches and cream. That near to her, Quinn could feel the heat coming off Allie's body and it washed over her, igniting the passion that had been smoldering in her core all evening. Quinn pulled her in closer, grazing Allie's lips with her own. The other woman moaned softly and closed her eyes. Quinn ran one hand across Allie's cheek, running through her hair and then using it to draw her in nearer. The kiss was needful, demanding. Quinn's tongue brushed her lips, craving, begging for entry. Allie's lips parted with a groan and then there was only that moment. Quinn felt herself melting into Allie, becoming one with her. Quinn's hands began to move, sliding over the soft silk of Allie's dress, finding and pulling down the zipper. She began to slide the dress off Allie's shoulders and couldn't seem to get it off fast enough.

Allie suddenly sat up, her breathing ragged and her eyes heavy with desire.

She smiled.

"If you rip this dress, I'll never hear the end of it. Let me."

Quinn shook her head and smiled.

"You're crazy." She rose off the couch and began to walk toward the bedroom, stripping off her clothes with each step. Quinn glanced over her shoulder at Allie, who was still seated. "Last one there…"

“And I’m the crazy one?” Allie asked grinning, then rushed by Quinn, pulling the dress off over her head and letting it fall to the floor in a heap.

They fell onto the bed, a tangle of legs and arms. Quinn kissed Allie along the cheek and neck, trailing kisses down her chest until she reached her breasts. With a sound that was almost a growl, she kissed along the edge of one breast and then licked the underside of it as Allie gasped for air, arching beneath her. Quinn covered one hardened nipple with her mouth and began to nip and suckle it as she traced her fingers lightly down Allie’s side. Moaning, Allie writhed beneath her.

Suddenly, Quinn felt Allie’s arms rise up and around her and then they were rolling. Allie knelt over Quinn with a knee on either side of Quinn’s hips. Allie looked down at Quinn and smiled.

“My turn,” she purred, and began to lick and kiss Quinn’s stomach. Allie moved up and mimicked Quinn’s actions, kissing and nipping at her breasts. When Allie began to circle one rigid bud with her tongue, Quinn felt the heat stoking low in her body begin to rise. She groaned and ran her hands along Allie’s back and shoulders, trying to bring her back up to Quinn’s lips. Allie smiled and shook her head.

“Mmmnnn, not going to happen. I said it was my turn.”

Allie lowered her head and then began to lap and nibble her way down to Quinn's stomach and hips. She continued down further still, her lips and tongue setting fire to Quinn's body with every touch. When Allie playfully bit the inside of her thigh, Quinn nearly came off the bed. She gripped the sheets and bit her lip, whimpering as she felt Allie's hot mouth at her mound. When Allie brushed over her clit, Quinn lost all coherent thought. Crying out in pleasure as Allie relentless flicked her tongue, Quinn thrashed on the sheets, grasping Allie's hair and wrapping her fingers around it.

"Oh God, Allie," she cried as the other woman gripped her hips and licked the length of her channel. Allie swirled her tongue around Quinn's clit, then drew it in between her lips, suckling and then flashing her tongue over it again and again. Quinn moaned as Allie slid first two and then three fingers inside her, thrusting in long, slow strokes. She pulled in a ragged breath when Allie replaced the fingers with her tongue. Quinn felt the world around her splinter as she began to shudder and spasm, losing herself as wave after wave of passion carried her away.

Slowly, she came down, panting as Allie crawled seductively up the bed until she lay side by side with Quinn. She smiled at Allie and wrapped her arms around her, pulling the other woman close. Allie gently pushed back a hair that had fallen across Quinn’s face and then nestled her head against Quinn’s neck, kissing the soft skin there.

“I would say that you are most definitely a prospect,” Allie whispered.

Epilogue

"I can't believe I let you talk me into this."

"Seriously, Rebekah? Are we really going to do this?" Quinn asked, dropping the last of the cardboard moving boxes into the kitchen.

Her sister sighed and crossed her arms.

"I'm just saying…"

"Just saying what? We've been over this. You need a real grown-up house, not some three room apartment. It's gonna kill you to live here and save me the hassle of trying to rent it out?"

Allie leaned back on couch and laughed at the exchange between the two sisters. At the sound, both Briscoe sisters stopped and turned to stare at her from the kitchen.

"Something you'd like to add here, Sugar Bug?" Quinn asked, raising one eyebrow.

"Uh…*Sugar Bug*?" Rebekah asked, wrinkling her nose. "Do I need to give you two some alone time or something?"

"No, I wouldn't, Quinn. And ignore your sister, Rebekah. She knows how I feel about that name," Allie said sharply. Allie hated to admit it, but deep down she got a little shiver whenever Quinn called her by her childhood nickname.

Quinn sighed and ran a hand through her short, honey-auburn hair. A sign, Allie had discovered over the past seven months, that she was getting annoyed.

"So, what is the big deal all of a sudden? We've been talking about this for weeks. You said you needed a bigger place. Allie and I are tired of making that drive back and forth to see each other all the time. You move in here, I move in with her. Now, what? You've changed your mind?"

"No, that's not it."

"Then what?"

"Well, it's that cat," Rebekah said, pointing to the calico cat that sat on the edge of the couch glaring back at her.

"The cat?" Quinn asked, shaking her head.

"Yes, the cat. I don't know why the cat can't go with you."

Oh hell, no.

Allie looked at Quinn and widened her eyes, shaking her head and mouthing the word "no". Quinn smiled back and nodded.

"Rebekah, this is the cat's home. I can't just ask him to up and move."

Her sister raised one eyebrow. "It's a cat, Quinn. I don't think you ask it anything."

"Rebekah…"

"Oh, okay. The cat can stay with me," Rebekah said, heaving a sigh. "But, you owe me."

"I'll get you a king sized pillow for your bed, how about that?"

Rebekah frowned.

"Why would I need that?"

"You'll see," Quinn said, eyeing the calico cat with a sly grin. "Allie, you ready to go?"

Allie jumped up from the couch, eager to the leave the house before Rebekah changed her mind about the cat. "Most definitely. See you later, Rebekah," she said, following Quinn out the front door and quickly down the front porch steps. As they reached Allie's Jeep parked in the driveway, Quinn suddenly stopped and looked back towards the house.

Allie walked up beside her, wrapping her arms around Quinn's waist.

"What are you thinking?" she asked.

Quinn had a wistful look in her eyes for a moment and then shook her head and smiled.

"Nothing. It's just been a long day. I think I'm ready to go home now, how about you?"

She looked at Quinn and felt a warmth settle across her chest. Allie leaned in and kissed her softly on the cheek.

"I can't think of anything else I'd rather do."

The End

The Scent of Jasmine

Four years ago Jessica Taylor thought she was ready to leave small town living behind and headed West. Now she's back in Cedar Creek, a little older, a lot wiser, and ready to live the quiet life for a while.

It's been eight months since her fiancée walked out and shattered Grace Donnelly's dreams of a happily ever after. Her friends tell her it's time to start living again, but the breakup with Emma was still just too raw for Grace to wash her hands and move on.

After a chance meeting at her brother's bakery, Jessica finds herself unable to get Grace off of mind. She's sure she feels an attraction from Grace as well, but will Jessica be able to convince Grace to stop living in the past and take a chance on a future together with her...

HURT

When it comes to matters of the heart, Nicole Landers has made some wrong choices. But now Nicole, one of the top real estate agents in Chattanooga, thinks she's finally made the right one in Jamie Tate. Despite a serious Johnny Cash obsession and a tendency to shy away from long-term commitment, Jamie seems to be the perfect choice. Jamie is kind, loving and especially nice to Nicole's elderly grandmother. Now all Nicole has to do is convince the attractive police detective that it's time to take things to the next level.

Jamie is crazy in love with Nicole and ready to move their relationship forward. Jamie decides it's finally time to sell her home and move in together—something that Nicole has been talking about doing for months. Knowing that Nicole believes her to be commitment-shy, Jamie thinks it might be fun to surprise her with the move.

However, things take on an ironic twist when an old friend Jamie hasn't seen in years comes by to look at the house, setting into motion a series of events that leaves more than just Nicole and Jamie's relationship in jeopardy.

About the Author

Lila Bruce lives in the North Georgia Mountains, where the air is sweet and the summers are hot. When not writing, she spends her time adding to her ever-growing pack of basset hounds and dreaming of being able one day to leave behind her evil day job.

Made in the USA
San Bernardino, CA
14 December 2016